Jack & Master

Karan Verma is a jack of all trades and master of some. A writer, entrepreneur and a prolific public speaker across B-schools, this young lad from Lucknow is a software engineer and a management postgraduate from IMT Ghaziabad. With television shows and a couple of films in his kitty, this debutant author seems all set to reach out for the stars.

Follow him at: twitter.com/karanverma_5
Contact him at: karanvermalko@gmail.com
For more updates on *Jack & Master*: facebook.com/jackandmaster

Jack & Master

A tale of friendship, passion and glory

KARAN VERMA

Published by
Rupa Publications India Pvt. Ltd 2014
7/16, Ansari Road, Daryaganj
New Delhi 110002

Sales centres:
Allahabad Bengaluru Chennai
Hyderabad Jaipur Kathmandu
Kolkata Mumbai

Copyright © Karan Verma 2014

This is a work of fiction. Names, characters, places and incidents are either the product of the author's imagination or are used fictitiously, and any resemblance to any actual persons, living or dead, events or locales is entirely coincidental.

All rights reserved.
No part of this publication may be reproduced, transmitted, or stored in a retrieval system, in any form or by any means, electronic, mechanical, photocopying, recording or otherwise, without the prior permission of the publisher.

ISBN: 978-81-291-3093-8

Second impression 2014

10 9 8 7 6 5 4 3 2

The moral right of the author has been asserted.

Printed at Shree Maitrey Printech Pvt. Ltd., Noida

This book is sold subject to the condition that it shall not, by way of trade or otherwise, be lent, resold, hired out, or otherwise circulated, without the publisher's prior consent, in any form of binding or cover other than that in which it is published.

To Mom
my mentor, guide and everything...

Contents

1. It Was a Tiger	1
2. Legacy or Moments	15
3. The Girl in the Binoculars	28
4. My Heart Is Beating	44
5. Jacked!	66
6. It Was a Straight Line!	82
7. And Then Began the Tough Part	90
8. Nirvana at 30	119
9. It Affects Us	135
10. It Affects Us–II	147
11. I High-fived It with My Heart	163
12. This Is My Yard!	175
13. The Bugles Had Been Blown	191
14. This Is Our Everest!	208
15. This Is It!	233
16. Master's Inner Thoughts	239
17. It Really Was a Tiger!	241
Acknowledgements	245

.1.

It Was a Tiger

Siddharth was generally not the kind of man who'd be swayed by the wind of exuberance and neither was he a person who'd bathe in a plethora of emotions, but then that day was an exception. Siddharth has always been poised and immovable like stillness in a frantic world. However on that day, he was so excited that he could barely sit still or hold a thought in his head.

Very rarely in one's life comes this day and when it does, you realize how vulnerable you are deep inside. It's only then that one discovers how badly one wants certain things in life and that no matter how much we keep telling others and ourselves that, "It doesn't matter whether I get there or not", the fact is, "Ah, hell it matters!"

As for Siddharth, well, he was still trying to come to grips with that day.

The occasion that day had opened the floodgates of so many memories and so many thoughts that it became difficult for him to separate the two. Emotions…thoughts…memories, his mind had become a free for all but then, what happened shortly was something magical. There came a moment when his mind rose above all the contemplations and deliberations and it started soaring fearlessly like an eagle with wings spread in blissful magnificence, with no emotions withholding, no strings attached. He had never in his life been at so much peace with himself and neither had he ever been as overwhelmed with a sense of satisfaction as he was at that moment.

Meanwhile as he assimilated his thoughts, there was something else soaring exactly the same way as his mind. It was our National flag. Not too many sights are more pleasant than the fluttering tri-colour at India Gate. That's where the stage was set. Siddharth had some fascinating memories of this place where he had come for the first time along with his father in his toddler days. Back then as a kid, he was absolutely fascinated to see the India Gate and the Parliament House. His sole motive then was to go back to school after vacations and boast of his visit to his friends and feel one up. Little did he know thirty years later he'd revisit the place in a totally different fashion for a totally different purpose.

Having roughly settled his partially grey hair he turned up the collar of his winter coat as the buzz of the gathered crowd began reaching audible levels. Backstage all he could hear was a set of unintelligible voices gathering steam. As the buzz kept getting more and more palpable one could sense anticipation—a build-up to something special. Guests were pouring in to attend this special occasion. Right from the Mayor of Delhi to the State Ministers, from the who's who of the industrial world to the political heavyweights…everybody had gathered at India Gate. As far as Siddharth was concerned, one could safely say it was perhaps the biggest day of his life. The unintelligible voices suddenly metamorphosed into a cacophony of thunderous claps as the event kick-started.

Amidst the applause and amidst the flashing shutterbugs, out came the announcer on the giant dais facing India Gate. With a glorious red carpet below and the arc lights above, everything from the couch and the podium to the on-stage gadgetry adorned the occasion, as the crowd braced for what was going to be one long evening.

'Ladies and gentlemen, welcome to the Hall of Fame ceremony,' declared the announcer who was the editor-in-chief of a famous news network. He exuberantly continued, 'Today, we celebrate achievement. We celebrate the spirit of those individuals who'll be inducted into this prestigious Hall of Fame. Individuals who've made us and this country proud. Without further ado, I'd like to call over the first inductee into the Hall of Fame this year.

'He is an economist par excellence. Having more than 250 research papers and over 100 publications, this man has chaired committees which have gone on to draft policies and legislations that have impacted not just our nation but the global community at large. He is an institution in himself. He seldom talks but when he speaks, everybody from the heads of the states to ministry officials to foreign diplomats just sit up and listen. Above all he's one man who has always stood by his conviction. Ladies and gentlemen, give it up for Mr Siddharth Rane, whom we all know as Master.'

Yes indeed, the moment had finally arrived. It was this moment which defined the catharsis of Siddharth's life as he walked towards the arena. He entered the main stage and stood there tall, both figuratively and literally. Standing there what he saw was the stuff even dreams aren't made of. Every single individual was standing and applauding him. Master... Master was the chant at India Gate. Was it the chant or the thunderous claps? Wonder what was more music to his ears. After being greeted by the guests of honour, he took his seat and tried to sink in the moment but honestly the buoyancy of joy in his heart kept it afloat for a long time. The flashing cameras, the ever inquisitive paparazzi and above all his family and friends—all could be summed up in one word, 'Glory'. Master was bestowed with the Medal of Honor by the Home Minster whose presence further glorified the event.

The presenter spoke from behind the podium, 'Ladies and gentlemen, there was a time when people used to vie and die for knighthood. They'd love to have a "Sir" before their names. Well, those who know this gentleman actually vie to become a Master rather than a Sir.'

Loud claps added to the compliments showered on Master.

The presenter continued, 'It's a proud moment, ladies and gentlemen not just for Master but for each and every one of us.'

'Sir, oh, I'm sorry, Master, I would request you to talk us through your illustrious journey. We are all eager to hear from you,' said the presenter.

The crowd once again greeted him with their generous claps. Master was too overwhelmed to speak but then that day, he was going to speak his heart out.

'Thank you everyone for your affection,' greeted Master in his characteristic baritone. 'The best thing about claps is that they don't discriminate. We are the country that gave to the world the sound of "Aum", pure and divine. For me the sound of your claps was as pure and as priceless,' he said, barely able to withstand the overwhelming rush of emotion.

The claps began pouring in again. Perhaps he wanted them to stop so that he could speak, but a part of him wanted to bask in the music of those claps forever. Regrouping himself he continued, 'Every morning when I get up I make a promise to myself, a promise to never compromise on my ideals. A promise that whatever I'll do, whatever I'll propose won't just be for the welfare of a single individual but for the welfare of the society, the welfare of the nation. It is this pursuit that's taken me through thick and thin, and all I can say is that I'm still walking.'

The gathering reverberated with thunderous claps again. The paparazzi, meanwhile, was itching to dig deeper and hear more from Master.

Challenges, controversies, hard fought battles, accomplishments, setbacks, not every day does one come across a life as absorbing and as grinding as this one. There were questions flying thick and fast, as everybody pressed for Master to talk them through the roller coaster of a life he'd had.

'I agree, it has indeed been a roller-coaster ride,' said Master with a smile. 'But today as I sit here on this coveted Hall of Fame couch, I must confess that the single biggest thing that brings a smile to my face is not the medals, not the research papers, nor the policy amendments that I could implement. It's the people I have met in my life,' he declared.

'Had it not been for the different people I met, the canvass of my life wouldn't have had a semblance of the colour and flavour that it has today,' he said, slowly looking around at the gathering as with a smile on his face, he saw images of different people flashing across his mind. The flashes continued for a while and so did Master's ponderous gaze.

Loosening the collar button of his navy blue shirt, Master said, 'You know the fascinating thing about life is that with the feverish pace at which it unfolds it doesn't really let you realize how significant or trivial a person is in your life.' Philosophizing further, he said, 'And today as I look around, I'm most happy to see that every person, every character that ever mattered in the theatre of my life thus far, is present here at this moment.'

The crowd was riveted by Master's narrative and the rivet just got tighter when he said, 'except for one'. The statement sent the gathering and the paparazzi into a frenzy as everybody waited on tenterhooks to know who the person was.

'Our journeys started at pretty much the same time. I always had a feeling that our destinies were written by the same pen, but perhaps with a different ink,' said Master. You could bet the man was getting warmed up for what was going to be one hell of an evening. The entire gathering was abuzz with inquisitiveness. Who was he? Where was he? Why did he matter that much to Master? The anticipation was building up.

'He's not here today and neither have I met him for quite some time, though I do hope to meet him soon. When and where, I have no idea, but I have faith that destiny will indeed make us meet pretty soon.' Marveling at their connection, he continued, 'Honestly we've never planned to meet—it has always just happened.'

'Sir, tell us more about the guy, who is he and why is he such a major chapter in your life?' enquired a journalist, echoing the question everybody sitting there had in their minds.

Hearing this, Master slipped deeper into the couch and took a walk down memory lane.

'Well, it all started some twenty years back in Goa—Grinnel's University, our alma mater, where my journey began, where our journeys started. It was here that I met this guy who was like a breeze of fresh air. His name was Jack.'

～

There was a young twenty-something boy, running full speed through the corridors of Grinnel's. Restless and effervescent, there was an impish sparkle in his eyes. His flying fore locks had a bounce similar to the spring in his strides as he rushed through the academic block. Pausing for a second, he inquired from the slightly old sweeper about the location of the economics department. He came running into lecture theatre-II of the economics department and said, 'May I come in, Ma'am.'

The person was so late that it was difficult to know whether he had been late for the current lecture or was too early for the next.

Now the lecturer, Mrs Franklin, although a very kind-hearted lady, had a characteristic sternness in her demeanour which was complemented by her grey hair and broad spectacles. She sternly asked, 'Is this the time to come to the class?' He was about to say something when Mrs Franklin interjected, 'And why the hell are you running? Is somebody chasing you or what?'

Everybody thought that he would sheepishly lower his head, say sorry and come in but what happened was something no one could have fathomed. He responded in a very surprised tone, 'Ma'am, how did you know?'

Mrs Franklin, even more surprised, said, 'You mean to say, someone was chasing you?'

'Exactly Ma'am, that's the reason why I'm late. I was actually chased by a tiger.'

Every student, at some point or the other in life has concocted different excuses—from missing a bus to traffic jams to falling ill, they've said and heard it all before but this tiger chasing excuse was outrageously original. No one could keep a straight face but he said it so nonchalantly.

'You mean to say you were chased by a tiger on your way here?' asked Mrs Franklin, trying to digest this.

'Exactly Ma'am, it was a tiger,' the boy claimed.

'And would you believe it, our battle was really intense and honestly, we were pretty well matched too.' He continued, 'The tiger was indeed ferocious but Ma'am, I must confess I'm even more ferocious.'

'Oh really!' exclaimed Mrs Franklin as if trying to figure out how she should react to this.

'Ma'am, I would've killed him but then my eyes fell on the words written on my T-shirt—Save the Tiger—so I left him and came running here.'

Everyone was in fits of laughter but this guy said it with a straight face though the mischief in his eyes was apparent. Even Mrs Franklin, in spite of her best efforts, couldn't avoid the smile on her face and asked him, 'What's your name?'

With an impish smile ready to break free from his eyes, he said, 'My name is Jack.'

'Take your seat, Jack and in the future, stay away from tigers,' said Mrs Franklin.

*

'Nobody had seen Mrs Franklin as such a sport but that's exactly the thing about Jack—he could win you over with the stupidest of things and you'd know that and still willingly fall for it. I, kind of liked him right from the start,' recalled Master.

*

The Principal called all the students over to Vasco Hall and briefed them about what was in store for them at Grinnel's. Grinnel's, at that time was indeed touted as the foremost college for post-grads—especially in economics. Getting into this coveted institute—was as tricky as solving a Rubik's cube in less than half a minute. There was no clear criteria. A high rank was no guarantee of selection. Students with a rank as high as 91 didn't make it, whereas Jack, having a profile as diverse as playing state level soccer to winning national level cyber competitions, had made it—despite his relatively lower rank of 293. As far as Master was concerned, he believed in keeping things simple. He was rank 1 in the entrance exams, period.

Ever since Master could remember, he had always wanted to be an economist. Not a rubberstamp run-of-the-mill economist, but an independent voice, free and powerful enough to change the perceptions of society. For Master, economics wasn't just a discipline or a vocation; it was something spiritual, something he was passionately in love with.

As far as Jack was concerned—his name said it all—he was a jack of all trades. He could play the guitar and sing his way into your heart and at the same time, he could also be a sub in your college soccer team. From writing some rustic, unconventional poetry to talking economics, he could pull off anything. He could charm Satan if need be and make you forget your worries even if it was just for a moment.

'Oh yes, we were quite different and so was our first meeting. I remember that day distinctly as ever. It was in the lecture hall "Yudhisthir", where one of our senior-most faculty on advanced macro-economics, Prof Bhaskar was giving a lecture,' recalled Master.

Prof Bhaskar, although a maverick in his field, was compulsively rigid and closeted to new ideas. He was an old school believer of statistical analysis and quantitative economics. Numbers for him were the language of economics.

It so happened that while discussing cost benefit analysis (a famous discipline of economics) Prof Bhaskar wrote down three questions on the board. Laptops aside, power-point slides aside, he was the conventional paper, pen, board and chalk kinds. Siddharth was absolutely consumed by the problems on the board. His pen was working at lightning speed, second only to his brain perhaps.

Prof Bhaskar, meanwhile was brain-storming over the questions.

Siddharth was oblivious to where he was or what he was doing. All he knew was that the third question had intrigued him like no other. So much so that he didn't react to anything around him. For those fifteen-twenty minutes, he was completely switched off from the rest of the world. However, what switched him on was not a finger-tip but a flying chalk finding its mark on his head.

Siddharth was up with a puzzled look and what followed was a furious reprimand by the professor. However, surprisingly or rather funnily it didn't elicit much of a response from Siddharth whose mind was still stuck at the third question. Suddenly, out of nowhere he cried out loud, 'Professor, the third question on the board is factually incorrect on many parameters.' Siddharth declared it as if it was a commandment. 'I can prove it, Sir and honestly thanks to this incorrect question, we get a lot of clarity on how resources can be better distributed,' said Siddharth while flicking through his worksheet.

Prof Bhaskar was livid. He shouted, 'Question is wrong. Oh, that's the shit you want to give me for not paying attention, you punk.'

'Sir, please see my paper. I think we can't confine this question to numbers and derivatives—it has many layers to it. We can't limit it,' said Siddharth as he tried passing his paper to the professor.

'You know what we can limit is your gibberish nonsense in this class. Just cut the crap and pay attention, will you?' scoffed Prof Bhaskar.

Siddharth was livid with the professor's outrageous behaviour and in a slightly assertive way he said, 'Sir, no amount of dismissive rhetoric from your side can justify question 3.' He was in no mood to give up as the duel had just gotten interesting. A stunned silence across the lecture hall added to the tension.

Siddharth passed his paper to the professor who reluctantly held it for a second before dropping it on his table in front.

'Sir, what I mean to say is...' continued Siddharth before he was interrupted again by an even more furious voice.

'You mean nothing, absolutely nothing,' fumed the professor, heightening the tension in the class.

'Nobody's interested in what you are saying,' he declared.

'Is anyone interested in what this chap is saying?' he angrily asked the class, completing a formality.

There was pin-drop silence in the lecture hall, till one heard a voice from a corner which said, 'Sir, I'm interested.'

Everyone in the class turned their heads to see who this I-want-to-commit-suicide person was. Well, it was Jack.

With a pleasant smile across his face, he was inquisitive to know Siddharth's version. Prof Bhaskar was irate. And for a while, all he did was give Jack a you're-dead stare. Jack's beaming smile however, didn't elude him.

The professor broke the silence by saying, 'Okay, fair enough.'

Now when a person expected to explode in anger talks rather calmly, you know you're in trouble.

'Since you are interested in this paper (picking it up from the desk) I suggest you take this and satisfy all your interests in life.' Saying this, the professor handed over the paper to Jack and asked him to get out of the class.

Jack said, 'Sir, but...'

'Out' was the single word that reverberated loud and clear across the class as Jack was on his way.

Question 3 seemed dead and buried for that lecture. However the I'm-interested boy outside the class kept it alive. He found Siddharth's paper interesting or whatever, but something struck him and he went to the head of the department.

A few minutes later Prof Mascranehas, who, by the way, was an internationally acclaimed economist, entered the class to everyone's surprise.

Prof Bhaskar greeted him and seeing Jack along with him, he thought the HOD had come to reprimand Jack. Prof Mascranehas asked Prof Bhaskar, 'Who has written this paper?'

Hey, that's my paper, thought Siddharth. Prof Bhaskar mockingly said, 'It's from a boy of this class, Sir.'

Siddharth stood up from his seat.

'Youngsters these days want to disprove things rather than proving them,' he added.

You could tell, for sure, that Prof Mascranehas wasn't an iota interested in Prof Bhaskar's outlook on today's youngsters. All he was interested in knowing was the thought behind the paper in his hand. For the next fifteen minutes, only Prof Mascranehas and Siddharth talked. Nobody coughed, nobody moved and nobody even sighed for those fifteen minutes. All that was heard was pure economical poetry.

'Out of my 250 research papers, that solution to the third question of Mr Bhaskar's lecture went on to become my first research paper.' A gentle string of claps by the crowd acknowledged Siddharth's first step towards becoming a master.

Prof Mascranehas declared the paper a path-breaking insight that could be worked on and modeled to reach somewhere concrete. He also declared that it'd be used as a case-study for the faculty itself. Prof Bhaskar, meanwhile, was frozen. Out of place would be an understatement.

As Prof Mascranehas was about to leave the lecture hall, happy and satisfied, Jack intervened and called out to him, 'Sir.'

'Yes,' said the HOD, with a screeching halt on his way out.

With a smile, Jack spoke, 'Sir, actually the entire credit of this goes to our lecturer, Prof Bhaskar. I can't tell you how encouraging he is to new ideas and discussions.'

'That there, was the stroke of the evening by Jack. Wonder what Jack was doing there? Was it a way of taking a dig at Prof Bhaskar or his way of befriending him and making him feel comfortable, one can't say.'

The HOD, however, showered praise on Prof Bhaskar for whom every word seemed like a bullet from a .303.

After the lecture ended, Siddharth went straight to Jack and before he could open his mouth and thank him, Jack shot back, 'Governance and economics? You gotta be kidding me. I don't buy that logic. But barring this last argument of yours, everything else in the paper was either bloody brilliant or I-am-too-bloody-amateurish.'

Master smiled and replied, 'I guess it's the latter. What do you say?'

Jack winked and said, 'Hmmmm....Me too. I mean, it can't be bloody brilliant, especially not when the paper stands for economists making good politicians.'

'Yeah, right. But don't worry, you'll gain perspective and be more than an amateur one day,' said Master, keeping the gimmick going.

'Oh really?' asked Jack with a smile.

'Aha,' Master replied.

'You know what was the best part?' said Jack.

'Which one?' asked Siddharth with inquisitiveness.

'The part where I told the HOD that it was all Prof Bhaskar's guidance and wisdom,' cracked up Jack.

'Hahahaha...' Siddharth also joined the laugh.

Jack chuckled, 'You saw his face there?'

Ripples of laughter ensued as Siddharth said, 'You really had him in a tough spot. Hahaha...'

'But you know what...' said Jack.

'What?'

'Economists don't make good politicians.' Jack's broken tape started again.

'Ah, come on. Amateur, you don't know that...'

'I'm telling you. Listen, you know that guy in Africa? He was an economist...' The two lovingly or, may we say, passionately, argued back and forth.

.2.
Legacy or Moments

The gathering at India Gate had a good laugh. Sharing their laughter Siddharth said, 'But it's not only that Jack had my back, I too was the butt-saver sometimes. I still remember that day...,' he smiled and continued, 'It was during Prof D'Costa's lecture on Dalton's Economic Theory where Jack as always was late.'

Prof D'Costa was a character you wouldn't find anywhere that easily. He was a visiting professor from Sweden and his face was the closest thing to Einstein's. But besides his Einstein looks, things that were even more apparent were his eccentricities. He was beyond the centuries old debate as to whether economics is an art or a science. He believed economics was pure magic.

Funny as it may sound, Prof D'Costa was as convinced about it as archaeologists were about radio-dating. He had taken his belief to a point where his lectures actually had the feeling of a magic show. He would bring multi-coloured plasticine balls with which he would create different shapes. A yellow ball would depict a consumer, a green one would be used to show an industrialist, orange would be something else and by the end of his magic show or lecture he would mix and match plasticine in such a way that a new colourful entity would be formed which he called "Magic". Prof D'Costa was within striking distance of achieving magic yet again when Jack slowly and stealthily arrived from the back door and sat on the vacant chair next to Siddharth.

Prof D'Costa gave them a look which said it all. His magical eye had perhaps noticed some sort of a difference as he kept looking towards Jack. Jack, though, unperturbed by his look wore a puzzled and engrossed look as if he had never heard a better lecture before.

'You were not here,' said the professor, as if trying to confirm.

Jack, as always, responded confidently 'Sir, I was here,' as if that was as obvious as the presence of gravity on Earth.

Prof D'Costa was in no mood to relent and he mockingly said, 'You mean to say you were here,' pausing at every single word.

Jack affirmatively said, 'Yes Sir, right here.'

None of them were ready to budge as the focus of all the students had now shifted from Dalton to Jack and D'Costa.

'Okay, fair enough. You say you were here, no problem. No problem at all.' D'Costa was getting more and more paranoid with every passing second. 'Tell me something about Mr Dalton and his economic views. You were here, you must've heard me.'

Jack stood up with a lot of hesitation and said, 'Of course, Sir. Your lecture on Mr Dalton was enlightening. In fact, I should say it was magical. As far as Mr Dalton is concerned.... Ah ah...' His eyes were rolling everywhere and his tongue just wanted to stick to something that could get him out of there.

'He was a great man. In fact, Mr Dalton was a very great man.'

'Then?' said Prof D'Costa as if ready to pounce on Jack.

'Sir, Mr Dalton was such a big man that I feel too small to talk about him. Sir, how can I speak about him?'

'I say you speak,' said Prof D'Costa firmly.

'Okay, Sir. I was saying, Mr Dalton is a…'

'Great man. Then what? Speak up,' insisted the professor.

'Okay, Sir,' said Jack reassuring him. 'Since you are insisting I'll speak, just for you, Sir.'

'Sir, we've heard and read so much about Mr Dalton, his theories etc. There are so many books and journals written about him. Nothing new but I'll tell you something really new and fresh about him,' Jack was building it up like a Hitchcock climax.

'What is that?' he asked.

'Sir, you'd be surprised to know that Mr Dalton actually knew a lot of languages. In fact, he even came to India once and said something in Hindi.'

'In Hindi?' the professor enquired surprisingly.

'Sir, he said *beedi jalaiyle jigar se piya, jigar ma badi aag hai*', Jack said, pronouncing every word slowly and surely, as if it was a theorem. Prof D'Costa obviously didn't understand it one bit. Siddharth was absolutely zapped and so was the rest of the class. It was hilarious and at the same time totally out of nowhere. The students were trying all sorts of things from clenching their lips between their teeth to stretching their facial muscles, but even their best efforts couldn't quite control the volcano of laughter which erupted every now and then in some corner of the class. Prof D'Costa was surprised at the reaction this so-called Dalton view had evoked. Never before had he seen the entire class react in such an extraordinary manner.

Curious to decipher this, he asked Jack, 'What is the meaning of this?'

Before Jack could speak further, something struck the professor and he asked Siddharth to tell him the meaning of what Jack had said.

'Now, all of us in life must have had a good laugh at some point or the other but trust me, in hindsight you'll always cherish the moments where you had to hold back your laughter. I was experiencing one such moment not aware that twenty years later I'd be recalling it the way I am. Coming back, somehow I managed to control my laughter and stood up to answer Prof D'Costa.'

He had absolutely no idea of what *beedi jalayile* meant. Siddharth looked at Jack in absolute disbelief—disbelief at what he'd just muttered. However Jack, one must say, was even then unfazed by the proceedings. He didn't say anything, though by his look towards Siddharth it was quite apparent that he wanted Siddharth to bail him out of this mud-hole. Siddharth's interpretation of *beedi Jalaiyle* would basically determine Jack's fate in the class. Pretty much like the professor, Siddharth too was clueless. Without thinking much he just started translating it and went with the flow.

He said, 'Sir, it's actually a very passionate appeal to young economic minds. In fact, so passionate that all I can say is one is smoking hot after hearing it.'

'Really?' asked the professor.

'Oh yes, Sir and also it's artistically metaphorical. I mean, it compares the economy of a nation to a cigarette i.e. *beedi*.' Letting his imagination run wild, Siddharth continued, 'And lighting this economy, is not a lighter or in our words a market force but the sheer fire in an economist's heart i.e. *jigar ma badi aag hai*.'

The moment had so much madness that the class didn't quite know how to react. One could bet they absolutely loved this economic axiom. Prof D'Costa was silent as were major sections of the class but then he said, 'It is indeed a magical thought.'

The class laughed and so did Prof D'Costa—who still didn't know what was so funny. Maybe cigarette, lighter and economics were a funny combination, he thought. The funniest part was when he said, 'It's actually one of the most thought provoking things I've heard in recent times.'

Siddharth could barely keep a straight-face and the brat that Jack was, he kept stoking the fire, 'Sir, there are so many layers to this thought, isn't it?'

'Actually,' thought the professor.

Jack got all the accolades from Prof D'Costa. In fact Prof D'Costa even tried to learn this line and Jack generously helped him in this endeavour. Every time Prof D'Costa tried to pronounce *beedi jalaiyle* the class cracked up like a house on fire.

However, the true volcano erupted when the lecture ended and the professor left. The class was literally rolling in laughter and you could bet they'd not laughed this hard in a long time.

'You're one crazy ass, Jack,' laughed Siddharth.

'My God, I can't believe what we did and by the way...' shouted Jack, as he stood on the bench.

'A round of applause for the gentleman,' Jack pointed towards Siddharth.

'I mean, if you can give "Beedi jalaiyle" a socio-economic

context then man, you're my Einstein,' clapped Jack and several other students in good fun.

'Next class...Kajra Re,' declared Siddharth, evoking even greater laughter.

'Now since it's raining songs in economics, how about we have some heavy downpour in the B-block hostel tonight?' asked Jack.

'Oh yes!' was the unanimous chant.

'And giving us company would be Beethoven, Mozart, Michael Jackson, of course the great Gulzar and yes, Birju especially for you, we'll have some Manoj Tiwari as well,' cracked up Jack.

Remembering those days, Siddharth smiled as he spoke from the heart, 'Today, I'm invited to the choicest of parties, five-star events, lounges, clubs and what not, but trust me, none of these hold a candle to the completely unapologetic savageness of a hostel party.'

It used to be a sight. If drinks and snacks were mere party appetizers, then the choicest of verbal expletives, light music and insane outpours of emotion were the desserts. The main grub, however, was the deliciously random talks bordering along professors-bashing to absolute trivial nonsense like why Birju keeps the toilet occupied for two hours every day to some elevated spiritual mumbo-jumbo like what really is life.

That night was no different and the boys at B-block were already in high spirits. Some of them, like Ankur, were feeling high enough and felt as if they'd broken free from their body.

'I'm a free soul' was the chant throughout the evening and indeed it seemed like he had been let free from somewhere. Siddharth, Jack and others were having fun, pumping up Ankur even more. If Ankur had risen above human bonds and tidings then Birju, his best pal, had nose-dived into a strange kind of rather funny emotional depth.

'Guys, you all are the only ones I have in this whole wide universe,' cried Birju with melodrama oozing out of every pore of his body.

'Ankur, I love you,' shouted Birju as he charged towards him in a topsy-turvy way.

'And I love humanity,' said a spiritually evolved Ankur with a straight face.

Jack, meanwhile was also quite a tanker contrary to a teetotaler Siddharth, who was laughing his heart out at the antics of everyone around him. Jack picked up his Jimi Hendrix-signed guitar and started crooning numbers from 'Summer of 69' to 'Purani Jeans' and some good old Ghulam Ali. Topping it all was the song written by him, 'Banjara'.

'Banjara main' was the chorus which echoed till late in the night as everyone, high or low, shouted their lungs out on that one.

Ankur, Birju and some others were singing and dancing in the aisles. They didn't care whether you played Bryan Adams or Ghulam Ali. Those boys had transcended the level of beat, rhythm and tempo. Music now lay within them and if they wanted to dance, they would, come what may.

Jack, on the other hand, was getting more creative as he could sing 'Banjara Main' on the tune of any popular song suggested by those around. From 'Jailhouse Rock' to 'Beedi jalaiyle', the Jack Banjara song could be moulded to fit every tune.

As the night ripened and reached its crescendo, the craziness and insanity gave way to some sorted and reflective talks. The music had become pretty light and the conversation slightly heavy.

'Nothing's forever, guys…nothing what so ever…' said Jack leaning backwards on his chair as he looked straight into the sky above.

'Except for what you leave behind,' came Siddharth's reply.

'Or what you carry with yourself,' reasoned Jack.

'You know what, Siddharth,' said Jack as he attentively sat forward on his chair. 'Years from now, when all this is done and dusted, all we'll remember are the moments. And God is the witness, I want to fill so much love, so much adventure, craziness, eccentricity, goodness, warmth and love in every moment, that it's etched in our memory…' he kept on speaking in one breath.

Everybody around either smiled sharing Jack's love for the moment or showered too much of reverence to pull his leg.

'Why don't I think like this?' wondered Birju in his typical naive manner.

'Anyway,' breathed out Jack.

'What do you want to leave behind?' he asked Siddharth.

'Legacy,' replied Siddharth in one word which said it all.

'It stays even after everything's gone,' he completed.

Jack smiled and so did the others and you could see respect written across their smiles.

'Legacy…moments…Oh my God,' shouted Jack to break out the heavy mould they had slipped into.

'I want to be a legend,' cried Ankur, from nowhere.

'Me too…Me too…' the chorus gathered steam. Jack and Siddharth laughed at the sudden return of madness in the lobby.

'Guys…,' shouted Jack, 'to be a legend, you have got to be a master of something…I mean born-for-it kinds, like Siddharth.'

Siddharth was a tad surprised and touched to hear what Jack just said.

'I mean, Siddharth and economics, look good together, man. He's born for it guys…they just…just look good together,' he reiterated.

'So do you and your guitar,' reasoned Siddharth.

'No…no…no…there's a difference. My guitar can look as good or even better with so many others. But you and economics Siddharth, are bloody synonymous,' nailed Jack.

'And that's why from today we'll call you Master,' winked Jack as very soon the 'Master' tag got attached to Siddharth.

*

'Oh yes, it was Jack who gave me the name 'Master' and since then it has stayed with me,' reminisced Master at the India Gate ceremony.

*

Amidst all the fun and frolic there was one silent spectator, sitting in the corner, quietly watching them with a smile. The affectionate smile across his wrinkled face exuded a lot of warmth and endearment. He was Joseph Perreira, popularly known as Good ol' Joseph amongst Grinnelites. The night watchman of the boys' hostel, both literally and figuratively. Master went over to his side and sat next to him. It was a matter of time before Joseph opened up to him.

'Son, I've been here for twenty-five years. So many kids like you have come and gone, right before my eyes,' said the old man.

'Where's your family?' enquired Jack.

The man smiled gently, even though the pain camouflaged under the smile seemed apparent. 'My son would have been your age, had it not been for the backlash in our village over a worthless piece of land,' Joseph painfully remembered. Over the next few minutes, Joseph narrated the story of how he lost his wife and only son in a rural feud some twenty years back.

'When I saw you guys singing and laughing together, I just got reminded of the song I used to sing for my wife during my hey days,' he smiled. And then in a rather impromptu manner, he started humming, 'My heart is beating…It's all repeating…I think of…' Good ol' Joseph sure won a lot of hearts there. And once he finished, Jack stood up and cheerfully declared, 'Stand back for the performer of the day,' as everybody cheered for Joseph.

'And, also today we have the newest member of our BC gang. Now please don't ask me what BC stands for,' laughed Jack along with the others as the party went on till early in the morning.

The next day, on an otherwise calm morning Master looked very rushed as he entered the Yoghurt Restaurant near Baga Beach with a bouquet of white lilies in his hand. As he entered he pulled a chair next to a lady who was sitting in casuals sipping a glass of water.

'Hi!' said Master with a smile. 'You seem to be waiting for someone?' he asked.

'Hmmm…Yes, I am actually,' said the woman whose large expressive eyes spoke so much that even a dictionary uttered at length would pale in comparison.

'Great!' exclaimed Siddharth with excitement. 'I'm also here for someone, for my girlfriend, you see.'

'Oh wow!' the lady exclaimed. 'What a coincidence. I'm also waiting for my boyfriend for the past two hours.'

Sharing her laughter, Master said, 'Oh, either he must be a fool or perhaps, must be caught somewhere. You never know.'

'Well, I'll prefer the fool part,' said the beautiful lady settling her spunky hair which had a bounce and fall similar to the one Jennifer Aniston had in the first season of *Friends*.

'Oh…let's leave the fool aside and have a coffee. What say?' said Master, placing the bouquet of lilies on the table.

'That's actually a good idea,' agreed the lady as she called out for the waiter extending her long slender arm.

'Excuse me, please get me one cappuccino and one black coffee with no sugar,' she ordered.

'Thank you,' said Master.

'I also brought these white lilies for her,' he said after an apprehensive pause.

'Nice. Aren't they?' he sheepishly enquired.

'But your girlfriend prefers roses not lilies,' asserted the lady.

'Oh…,' he sighed ruefully, waiting for the black coffee.

As the coffee was served, the lady very gently asked, 'So, what took you so long?'

Master smiled hesitantly and said, 'Honey, it had got very late in the night and then we hardly slept. So…' Fumbling for words, Master seemed really guilty as he looked around for a second and then, very innocently, just spoke up straight, 'Ah, I…I'm really sorry, Sakshi.'

The lady smiled radiantly and gently placing her hand on Master's palm, she winked at him and said, 'It's okay!'

'The way you just completely own up and say sorry always melts me,' she said rather lovingly.

'Well, if my sorry makes you smile, then I don't mind saying that all my life,' smiled Master.

'Hmm, that seems a smart strategy.'

'Well, can't blame your guy. He's an economist,' winked Master.

'And if people around him are to be believed, he's all set to have his first research paper published,' he declared.

'Aha…Research papers. That's a start,' she said, cheering him up.

Everything about Sakshi—from her eyes to her gestures to her touch—exuded so much warmth, so much affection, that a man would willingly barter his priciest material possession for a life-partner like her.

'Hey listen! How do you find this T-shirt?' asked Sakshi, in a characteristic girly-girl manner flaunting her attire.

'Awesome…in fact can I just say it's beyond words,' piped up Master.

'Who got it, honey?' he curiously enquired.

'Well, a guy named Siddharth got this for me,' came her deadpan reply.

'Ah…right, I know. Just wanted to check,' Master said with a lot of confidence. 'You know nothing,' spelled out Sakshi nonchalantly. 'You don't even remember that today is your parents' marriage anniversary.'

'Oh crazy…I completely forgot, Sakshi. Now what?' freaked out Master.

'Don't worry,' she said with an assuring smile. 'Look what I got for uncle and aunty,' said Sakshi, passing over a home-cooked pineapple cake she had made specially for them.

'Sweetheart, that's amazing and hey thanks,' said Master.

'They'll be really happy if we pay them a surprise visit.

Come on…, let's go,' said Sakshi as she in her characteristic enthusiasm got up and dragged Master along.

The two grabbed a taxi and headed over to Master's home.

Sakshi was welcomed with open arms by Mr and Mrs Rane. They hugged their son and even though they were not the type who wore their hearts on their sleeves, one knew they were extremely proud parents.

Master's parents didn't have a child till twelve years after their marriage before they got home a little boy from the Goa Foundation and Welfare of Orphans Association. This little boy had today grown up to be a handsome young man who many thought would be the next big thing in economics. Sakshi was personable and warm as usual. She had seamlessly merged with Master's family.

The candles were blown, the cake was cut and there was indeed bonhomie in the household. Sakshi always had so many incidents and so many stories to share that if one day she compiled those pieces together it'd make for a better thriller than Hitchcock's. Not to miss her impact-enhancing pauses and jaw-dropping special effects. For Master, she was pretty much the woman of his life, the woman who knew him from the time he couldn't correctly tie his shoe-laces, the woman who knew that the only coffee he had was without any milk and sugar.

.3.

The Girl in the Binoculars

It was one of those perfect pleasant weekends in Goa, where one could just bask in the glory of the city. The wanderer in Jack had absolutely unleashed itself. Casual shorts, slippers, binoculars in hand and a whistle on his lips, the boy was effortlessly flirting with the city, when suddenly his eye stumbled across something that caught his imagination. Boy! He suddenly realized that his binoculars were the best thing he had ever shopped for in his entire life. They were showing him something or should it be said, someone, who might just turn his world upside-down.

That someone was a young lass straight out of a Hollywood movie. Her shades, her leather bag, her accessories, everything was so crisply executed that it seemed she was one of those rare specimens preserved to show the world what style truly is. For a minute Jack couldn't hear the honking sound of the vehicles; the hustle-bustle of the marketplace didn't matter, nor did he hear the people around him. All he could hear inside his head was the yesteryear Michael Jackson scorcher, 'The way you make me feel'. This Michael Jackson number was doing lots of mumbo jumbo in his upper storey.

Crossing the four-lane highway down to the stoned roadside marketplace and finally through the sand across the beach side, Jack was just moving towards her. He didn't care whether he was disrupting traffic or crossing roads from the wrong side, he was just chasing the girl in his binoculars.

To the bystander it seemed, as if a lunatic had just seen the 'Airline to Heaven' through his binoculars and was chasing it before it gets full.

The trumpets were blowing and the song, 'The way you make me feel' had reached its penultimate crescendo in his mind as Jack, somehow in one piece and without much anatomic damage, reached the lady.

Jack was literally frozen when he saw her infront of his eyes. He said to himself, 'If she is God's creation then God has to be a sculptor.'

The darting movement of her eyes; the subtle and almost nimble movement of her hands; her long pointed nose elegantly poised on her angular face; her every single contour seemed perfect, except for that one flying flick of hair which had managed to escape from beneath her ear only to be leisurely flirting with her dimpled cheek right down till her neck.

With bated breath, Jack said, 'Hi!'

The girl replied, 'So here you are! Ha, what about the time? I've been waiting for you.'

A smitten Jack said, 'Well, I've been waiting for you all my life.'

'What?' exclaimed the lady. 'It looks like you are not in your senses.'

'You're to be blamed for that,' smiled Jack.

'Guess you need a life,' asserted the lady.

'Well! I just got one and trust me, I won't let it go easily.'

'Whoa…Okay…Okay…I mean, you were supposed to be here at 10. You turn up at 12 and then you talk strange. What's the matter with you?'

Jack had no idea what was going on. The lady was talking to him as if they had studied in high school together.

'You are so unprofessional! You had promised me that you'd cover all the beaches by evening and we haven't even started. It's because of guys like you that nobody is able to follow any schedule or plan things in advance. You deserve to be sued. What sort of responsibility do you guys have... Ha...You guys are a horrible example of the tourism of this state. I mean as a travel guide you should've been...blah... blah...blah.'

Jack was reprimanded by a woman he didn't even know five minutes back.

'Binoculars in your hand don't make you a travel guide.'

'Me, a travel guide? Wow! She actually thinks so...,' thought Jack.

The lady's rant continued, 'You should've known in advance...'

'Woah...woah...woah,' exclaimed Jack, amazed by the frequency at which the woman was speaking. She literally had Jack packing his bags and leaving the town.

'Ma'am...as your travel guide...' Fumbling for a second on 'travel guide' he continued with confidence, 'as your travel guide, I'm really sorry for being late. But, there's a reason why I'm late,' he said rather mysteriously.

'And what's that?' asked the lady.

'You see on my way here, an accident took place,' said Jack.

'What happened?' asked the lady with concern.

'I was on my bike, when it collided head-on with a double-decker bus on the way,' stated Jack.

'Oh my God!' she shrieked, looking at Jack from top to bottom, probably surprised at not finding any bruises or scars.

'Your bike into the bus...God, it must be shattered to pieces?' asked the lady.

'Well, it's in pieces, smaller than my little finger,' said Jack in a cheeky yet serious manner.

'And what about that bus and the driver?' she worriedly asked.

'I just told you it's in pieces,' came Jack's reply. The lady's mouth just opened up wide instantly. It was the sort of unabashed and unapologetic nonsense she hadn't heard in ages.

'You mean to say (clearing her throat) that the double-decker bus was reduced to pieces after colliding with your bike,' said the woman, trying to digest this.

'You see it matters who is riding it. If I am in the rider's seat, things like this are pretty normal,' claimed Jack with an absolutely straight face.

'Aha, I see,' said the lady, concealing and curbing the avalanche of laughter rearing to come out.

'Leave that, you tell me why are you waiting for the travel guide? I mean, me (with a hesitation) here in the middle of the road?' asked Jack.

'No...no...no, you got that wrong. You see I was actually waiting for you at the corner of the road. But then, the earth revolved and I reached the centre,' said the lady with a wry smile.

'I see,' nodded Jack with a smile, trying hard to remain normal after what he'd just heard. 'Must have been a great feeling...Ha?' he asked.

'Yeah, pretty much the same way you felt after reducing that bus to pieces,' quipped the lady.

Jack's smile was now reaching his ears. The lady too couldn't control her laughter—the floodgates opened and the two burst out laughing.

'Oh my God! I haven't laughed like this for a while,' said the lady.

'My sides are aching…hahahaha,' laughed Jack.

'So are mine,' as she gasped for breath amidst bouts of laughter.

The two literally sat down on the road and were rendered powerless by their incessant laughter.

Catching his breath, Jack extended his hand and said, 'Hi! I'm Jack.'

'I'm Samantha. Pleased to meet you,' the lady replied, shaking hands with Jack.

'Well Samantha, this is just the beginning. Brace yourself, because Jack and Goa are a toxic combination.'

'Aha! Really, Jack. What's so special about Goa?' asked Samantha with exuberance in her voice.

'Well, Goa is the second best tourist spot in the country,' claimed Jack.

'And which is the first?' she asked.

'It's Goa, but only when you see it with Jack,' he replied with a wink.

Samantha smiled and tapped on his head as the two together started walking towards Calangute beach.

'I've been romancing this place ever since I remember,' said Jack.

'You've always been here?' Samantha asked.

'Yeah born, brought up, studied, failed—everything for me has happened in Goa. Every street, every place here has its own story to tell.'

'Hey Mac, I'm fine. How're you doing?' said Jack responding to a greeting from a passerby. 'Miss your cookies, Mr Fernandez.' He cheerfully greeted everybody he met.

Surprised at Jack's popularity, Samantha asked, 'So, what are you Jack, a local folk hero or just a travel guide who seems to have a lot of takers here. Ha?'

'Na…Honestly, I don't know who I am. In fact, there are times I just don't want to know who I am. I'm just Jack you see…,' Jack continued smilingly, 'and right now Jack's a kick-ass travel guide.'

'Interesting, Mr Jack…So, in short, you're a wanderer, right?' confirmed Samantha as the two walked down the beach side.

'You can call me that,' said Jack.

'Wandering around Goa with Mr Wanderer. How cool does that sound?' asked Samantha.

'Cool enough to get you a dozen comments and maybe a dozen more likes on Facebook,' replied Jack.

Samantha smiled and asked, 'Yeah right! So, for how long have you been a travel guide?'

'Na, I wasn't really a travel guide a while back but then I met somebody who turned my world upside down,' said Jack.

'Okay, hope that somebody is really good,' smiled Samantha.

'Oh! You can bet on it,' he said, with an impish grin. He continued, 'By the way, what do you do, Sam?'

'I'm a fashion designer, mostly contemporary thus far, though I'm planning an ethnic collection also pretty soon… Fingers crossed,' she confidently said.

'That's cool. So now I know where your sharp dressing is coming from,' complimented Jack.

'Hmm,' smiled Samantha. 'By the way, don't forget to take me to some pearl or stone shop here. I heard they are really good…I've got to take some for my friends.'

'There's a better place down south…We'll catch that up…

Really you know someone there…No, someone there knows me…Hahaha…You are soooooo…Amazing right…'

Jack and Samantha continued their chit-chat right until they reached a local fair organized in front of Calangute Beach.

'Hey Jack! That's one of the local fairs right?' asked Samantha.

'Oh yeah! These fairs are a very common thing in this part of Goa.'

'Then let's go there,' said Samantha as she hurried to the fair dragging Jack along.

The fair was pretty much a 'Theatre of Dreams' sort of spectacle. Light, music, games and a whole lot of fun and razzmatazz decorated the extravaganza.

'You know Samantha, I must've been eight when my dad took me to one of these fairs for the first time. Mom, Dad and I had so much fun at all these games.'

'They indeed are a lot of fun, Jack. Look at that…where are all these people running and going?'

'Wait just a second. You know what, this is the Amazing Race that they're running for,' exclaimed Jack.

'It's a…uh…uh…' so excited was Jack that he was fumbling for words to complete his sentence. And then excited as hell he loudly exclaimed, 'Will you run this race with me, Sam?' The school boy in him was ready to charge.

'I don't have a clue about it Jack,' said Samantha whose adventurous side was itching to say yes without knowing anything.

'Yes or no,' shouted Jack with exuberance.

'Yes,' shouted back Samantha rather instinctively as she ran along with Jack to participate in what was a traditional Goan adventure race—The Amazing Race.

A roll of the drums kick-started the adventure. Jack shouted out loud, 'Run Sam...Run' as they both grabbed each other and ran as if it was the only way of survival left for mankind. 'Woohooo,' laughed Samantha as she hysterically ran with Jack. They both were in the midst of confusion, competition and hysterical laughter which had no reason. Together they went through mini water lakes, different slides, pie-eating contests and what not.

After a couple of hours of hell-raising and edge-of-the seat competition, the two were in striking distance of winning it. Shouting their lungs out with fun, they came down the giant water slide. Fun, nervousness, adrenaline, everything was happening as they went for the final dash of the race...And then their jubilation reached an apex when they crossed the finish line and won the Amazing Race.

For a shopaholic like Samantha, the prize was an absolute beauty. Jack and Sam were given a minute and a fixed budget to wrap up whatever they desired at the Calangute market. Both had their wish lists ready. Jack wanted to grab some beers and goodies whereas Sam's fashion designer eye was salivating for a flamboyant Lady Gaga dress.

'Sam, you gotta be a weirdo to like this dress. And by the way, this one dress will finish off our budget,' said Jack rearing to go inside for the minute.

'Fine Jack, have your way then. I'll wait outside,' said Sam in a resigned tone.

Jack, meanwhile, was too excited and starry-eyed to notice Sam's resignation. With eyes glued on packs of beer and goodies he said, 'Fine Sam you wait outside, I'll get something and then we can split. Get set go...'

Like a child who didn't get her favourite toy, Sam waited

outside for Jack.

'Whoa, now that's what you call one crazy ride,' exclaimed an excited Jack coming out after a minute with a couple of beers in his hand.

'Hey Sam, here you go, grab one Jack-weiser or should I say Sam-weiser,' said Jack, passing her a beer.

Sam sportingly smiled and said, 'Jack, I don't drink so you can have all the beer and pass me something else you got for me.'

'God, don't tell me you don't drink. That's all I really got for you,' said Jack, surprised.

Samantha smiled and said, 'It's okay, the kind of fun I've had today, I believe I got my prize.'

'Yeah right,' exclaimed Jack. 'But hey, there's just one little thing I got for you.'

'What?' asked Sam.

'Oh hang on I just left it inside, wait a second,' Jack rushed back in. A minute later Jack came out smiling with a small shopping bag. Placing the bag against his leg, he opened it up and out came the Lady Gaga gown.

Samantha's joy knew no bounds. Pleasantly surprised she couldn't stop smiling.

'Jack...,' she whispered, excitedly holding on to the dress. 'That must've completed the entire budget,' she realized. 'What about you Jack?'

Jack winked and seeing her all smiles he said, 'Well, I got my prize.'

'Hmm...Having said that, the pack of beer actually cost me a bomb,' chuckled Jack.

Sam laughed out loud and said, 'Don't worry, they'll come in handy.'

'Well, add my friends to it and it'll be more than just handy, it'll be one hell of a beer bash and that's why the bomb's worth it,' he exclaimed.

The two of them continued chatting as they walked down towards Baga beach.

'By the way Sam, how is your younger kid doing in school?' asked Jack out of nowhere.

Sam's jaw dropped open like a tiger's in front of its prey. On the verge of chewing off Jack, she said, 'Do I look like a mother? And younger kid in school? I wonder how big the older one is, according to you?'

'Relax, I didn't know that you guys didn't start a family even after being married for so long,' said Jack.

'Have you freakin' lost it, Jack?' shouted Sam.

'Now don't tell me you're not even married,' said Jack rather excitedly.

'I'm not,' she clarified.

'You're single, ready to mingle,' Jack cried out loud with jubilation.

'I'm engaged,' replied Samantha.

Dammit, shouted Jack in his head as the excitement fizzled out in a second.

'There you go, couldn't you have said it straight up,' said Jack.

'My God, couldn't you have cut all your younger kid, college jazz and asked me up front?' Samantha replied, wondering what had gone wrong with him.

'Anyway...So what's he like?'

'Well, he's Aakash from Mumbai. He's an investment banker. Just did his MBA from Yale.'

'Impressive resume. Don't have anything for him right now,

will get back to you if there is an opening, thanks,' piped Jack.

'You're welcome,' smiled Samantha.

'And when are you guys planning to get married?' asked Jack.

'Early next year, February probably,' she replied.

'That's like light years...I mean, are you sure, you guys are still going to be together till then?' said Jack with a casual smile that didn't really go well with Samantha.

'Oh I am sorry, but why did he not come along? I mean, it's a weekend, he could have just dropped in,' pointed out Jack in a suppressed tongue-in-cheek tone.

Samantha first wore a disgusted look but soon that disgust melted and gave way to a realization of sorts. Jack, who was dreading a showdown, smiled and cheerfully said, 'I got you thinking.'

'Yeah, I mean, he had work but he could have come,' he said.

'I need a break but...,' paused Samantha.

'But you love him,' said Jack, trying to cement things.

'Do I?' said Samantha.

Jack knew he had set the wrong ball rolling. 'Of course, that's why you guys are engaged,' smiled Jack.

'You are right. I must be in love, that's why I'm engaged,' reasoned Samantha.

Jack said, 'Must be,' giving her a thumbs up.

'Must be,' she thoughtfully and slowly exclaimed.

'But hey, why "must be", we "are" in love. What the hell is "must be" doing here?' she cried out loud.

I bet she is thinking hard and I bet she is freaking out a bit, thought Jack.

'Fine,' he said. Articulating it loud and clear he enunciated,

'You guys are engaged so you must be in love. Oh I'm sorry. Sorry, I'll say it again. You guys are engaged so you "are" in love. Happy?'

'Yes, that's better,' said Sam as they started walking again. After a couple of steps she stopped and said, 'Hey, this also doesn't sound right, does it? We are engaged and so we are in love...No. It should be the other way. We are in love and so we are engaged.'

Jack could sense that if they didn't get over this, it would be a looooong day.

'Oh it's nearly the same, just some subject-predicate grammar stuff, that's it. Let's see this place,' he said, diverting her attention.

'No, it's not the same,' Sam freaked out as her phone rang.

'Some divine intervention at last,' thought Jack.

'And guess what, it's the love of my life, Aakash, calling,' cheered up Sam.

She picked up the phone and then with her voice coated in sucrose, glucose and fructose she said, 'Hey sweetie, how are you doing?'

'You know what, I just realized, we are engaged and so we must be in love. Sorry, sorry, I mean, we must be engaged so we are in love.' Sam's goof ups kept getting more and more convoluted and funny as Jack helplessly saw the conversation fall apart like a pack of cards.

'No...no, I wasn't asleep or anything,' laughed off a confused Samantha over the phone.

'You know what, we love each other like crazy...Period... Matter ends,' exclaimed Samantha. She put the phone down but the conversation in her mind didn't stop. Awkward and a tad embarrassed, she told Jack, 'Okay, so, show me Goa...

Show me everything that's your job…Okay.'

'Of course…By the way, if I am not mistaken right now here at Cavelossim beach, we must be or rather we are standing at Goa's most beautiful place,' said Jack.

'No Jack, be clear. We "must be" or we "are" at the most beautiful place?' asked Sam. Ah how Jack wished these two words never existed in the English language.

'I can't really say,' replied Jack.

'Why dammit? Why you are not sorted out? It's high time you had an answer,' Samantha got all frantic and animated. Probably more than Jack, she was talking to herself. 'Look at me, I am clear…I say I am in love with Aakash not I "must be" in love with Aakash.'

'Yeah right, wish I had that clarity,' replied Jack. 'Aakash is a lucky man, I mean he has such a sorted fiancé…I mean who gets such a clear and sorted fiancé in today's world.'

Samantha cheered up and said, 'I swear! You know what, that makes me feel much better.'

'Thank God. And you know what else is clear today, the weather here, so let's go to some more places before it's cloudy again,' said Jack metaphorically as the two boarded a city bus.

After a long, happening day, the two came back and sat down at Cavelossim beach. The blood-gorged rays of the setting sun on the calm sea, seemed like phosphorous streaks. Bare feet on the sand, the cool breeze, the ambience and the sight, all of it was so calm and fulfilling that for about a minute both Jack and Samantha didn't say a word.

'Phew, that's pretty much it,' smiled Jack.

'Oh Jack, this has been my best trip in the last year,' claimed Samantha.

'Wow, that's the best compliment one could receive,

knowing that this has been your only trip in the last year,' quipped Jack.

'You never stop, do you?' asked Samantha.

'Not before the other one stops,' replied Jack.

With a heavy heart and a soft tone, Samantha said, 'It stops here, Jack.'

She held Jack's hand and continued, 'Jack amongst all my childhood memories, know which are the days I still remember…?'

Jack smiled and wondered as Samantha continued, 'I remember the day when for the first time I rode my bicycle in the third standard without my dad by my side and without those silly supporters. Know what else I remember? I remember the days when our entire family, cousins and uncles and aunts, used to go together for a family picnic. I also remember my parents' twenty-fifth anniversary. We had a blast! The day when everyone, my parents and my grandparents clapped for me when I became a small tree in a junior college concert and with all these days Jack, I'm going to remember today. Thank you so much for giving me one of those precious moments Jack.'

'Come here, Jack,' called out Sam, extending her arms.

'Woo…I…I mean,' fumbled Jack as he went and sat by her.

Jack couldn't say anything after repeated attempts. 'Jack, wasn't there something really exciting and rare in this day?'

Jack held her hand and with a smile said, 'Samantha for me that excitement, that madness is there in every moment. That's how I live, girl.' They both smiled as Samantha planted a gentle kiss on his cheek.

Rifling through her handbag, she asked, 'How much do I give you Jack?'

'Ah...ah...let me think,' said Jack as he tried to figure out.

'Come on, how much?'

'Was just estimating the price, turns out I'm priceless,' he said.

Sharing the laughter Sam said, 'Don't have that much.'

'Actually you do...,' said Jack, as a wave of excitement got him up and standing.

'What do you mean, Jack?'

'Look, Samantha...sit,' pausing for a second, he continued, 'I am not a travel guide.'

'What are you saying?' she wondered.

'I was just a passer-by who you thought was a travel guide. And then I thought hey, I'd actually rock as a travel guide. So...,' he explained.

'Oh my God...Oh my God,' she cried out.

'Ya, that's twice,' said Jack.

'My God, Jack...as much as I want to kill you for lying and kill my guide who didn't turn up, I must say you're a kick-ass travel guide. What do you do then?' exclaimed Samantha.

Jack smiled and said, 'Well, I'm a student at Grinnel's, an economics student, to be precise.'

'Oh, fantastic. So, you're a nerdy economics student and I thought I was with this adventurous wanderer who's a cool travel guide,' she wondered.

'Hmmm, I guess that's also another side of me,' he cheerfully said.

Sam nodded and then very affectionately said, 'Tell me Jack, what do you want for this day? I really want to give you something in return for the very special time I had today.'

'There actually is some thing you can do for me,' he said.

'Tell me.'

'I'd love to have you as my partner for the prom night at Grinnel's.'

Samantha, with her mouth wide open said, 'Jack, I'm engaged.'

'Now I'm not telling you to dump this guy and run away with me…am I?'

'But Jack…,' she said.

'I mean, just for one night, Sam,' he said.

'One night.' Jack, with his hand on his head said, 'I mean prom date for the night.'

Barely able to hold his laughter he exclaimed, 'You thought…'

'Shut up, will you.'

'Of course, of course,' he sheepishly said, anxiously waiting for her reply.

Samantha's face wore a puzzled look and after waiting for a while she said, 'But there is one problem, Jack.'

'One? That's a manageable number. What's that?' asked Jack.

'I don't really know how to dance,' she confessed.

'Ah, that's it?' he laughed.

'It's a major thing, Jack. I mean, I get really embarrassed.'

Jack went closer to her, looked her straight in the eye and passionately said, 'Sam, I promise you that if you come over, we'll have a dance that'll make the floor proud.'

'Ah…mmmmm,' she pondered.

'You know what, keep this card, that's my college invitation for the prom night. Decide whether you want to come or not. The floor will be waiting for you. See you.'

With these words and hope in his heart Jack waved goodbye and whistled along his path.

.4.

My Heart Is Beating

Back in the college, the preparations for the college fest were on in full swing. Besides the preparations, there were also regular classes, guest lectures and a whole load of matchmaking sessions for prom night. In fact virtual matchmaking would happen every night over drinks in the boys' hostel. Grinnel's wasn't too liberal with regards to drinking in the hostel. But courtesy the ever so lovable good ol' Joseph, the boys didn't have much to worry about. High on hope, Ankur openly declared his prom night plans.

He shouted, 'I will ask Sneha out for prom night, yohoohoo.'

Birju interrupted, 'What are you saying? I will ask her out. We look good together. Look at this…' He handed him a photo-shopped snap of him and Sneha together in the snow field of the Vatican.

'Brilliant, but take a look at this,' said Ankur, as he put forward another morphed photo in which he and Sneha were standing inside the torch held by the Statue of Liberty. They both asked Master, 'Who do you think makes a better pair with Sneha?'

'Hey, why don't you guys solve it right now,' suggested Master.

'How? Tell me,' enquired Birju, gulping down the last drop from the soda bottle.

'Mail her the two photos and let her decide who her man is,' fired Master in good fun.

Everybody rooted for the idea and shouted in unison 'Mail her! Mail her!' A complete craziness had gripped the dormitory. Master's jibe actually made these two cloud nine flyers think about doing this.

In fact they were about to mail the two photos to the entire group email id and ask for votes.

'Let's go the democratic way,' declared Ankur.

'All right, stop!' intervened Jack who seemed to have had enough of this.

Pausing for a second, he said, 'How can you go for voting? First let's have the canvassing, guys.'

Everybody shouted and laughed. The night seemed to be getting younger as the hostel terrace kept getting packed to the rafters.

'Okay, Birju, let's start with you. Why do you think, you're the man Sneha should go out with?'

'Because a man who can stand on his feet after ten drinks will always be standing by her,' claimed Birju.

Shouts of 'Wow…wow…' followed by loud whistles echoed through the terrace.

'Now if Birju is a great lady-killer, wonder what Ankur is. It's your turn now,' called Jack, keeping his drink aside on the Sintex water tank.

'Hey, but before that, let's take some tips from a guy who has perhaps done it all—Master,' called Jack.

Everybody looked towards Master as he just smiled and said, 'What guys? I have never said anything of that sort to Sakshi.'

'Ah come on, be a sport and share,' said Jack.

'Jack, I am serious. I have never felt the need. All I know is that we being in love with each other and wanting to spend our lives together is obvious.'

'No, that's where you missed the point. It ain't done till it is actually done. You have to propose to her,' said Jack, as he excitedly walked across the parapet to talk to Master up front.

'Oh, it's not required, Jack,' Master replied convincingly.

'It is,' said Jack.

'Not,' Master completed the sentence.

'It is,' reiterated Jack.

'Is it?' asked Master with a complete change in his tone.

'Yeah, do it,' suggested Jack.

'Oh, it's easy. There's nothing much,' assured Master.

'Is it?' asked Jack, aping Master's tone to pull his leg.

'No, it's not. I tried like a thousand times but couldn't do it. Dammit,' shouted Master, completely freaking out.

Jack started laughing and so did the entire bandwagon.

'Well, I must confess here that though I've been witness to some great times both professionally and personally but none of them compare to the time I had at Grinnel's. There was something so happy, so vibrant about that boys' hostel that it always felt like home.'

Grinnel's had a legacy of being host to some exquisite conclaves where great minds came together. This year's conclave centered on the economic condition of Goa and one of the chief guests included the State Planning Commission's Chief, Mr Vincent Nazareth.

The attendance registers clocked a huge turnout, though honestly, had there been a mental presence register, then only a handful would've seen a tick against their names. Amongst that handful there was one individual who for that hour, that moment, brushed aside all 'should I propose to her, should I not propose to her' thoughts, just to hear and see his passion unfold right in front of his eyes.

Mr Vincent Nazareth, well read as he was, had an air of smugness around him. He had an I-know-it-all attitude and also a brashly dismissive style, though many also believed that his bark was actually sharper than his bite. Master meanwhile had been quite closely scrutinizing the statements Vincent made. After a round of addresses by the chief guests, the house was open for a Q&A session. No hand except one was raised. Master grabbed the microphone, ready to ask the question, 'Good morning Sir. I have been following you closely and what I just realized is that your statement today is in complete contradiction with what you told the *Financial Times* on 19th June.' To everyone's surprise, Master categorically stated the earlier statement.

A man of Vincent's self-esteem, or should we say ego, didn't take it too well and literally went the rough way.

He dismissively said, 'Kid, you first need to get your basics right. Neither do you understand the subtleties of my policy nor do you have profound knowledge of the subject.'

'Sir you must be right,' acknowledged Master. 'I perhaps still have a long way to go but all I really want to know is, how come in two months, the R&D initiative of the state gets significantly less spending than it was promised and how even today, in spite of all the inflation and raised WPI's, the labour wages do not get a hike. Pardon me Sir, but aren't these government's double standards?' shot back Master.

'Look, you can't generalize things like this,' said Vincent. 'All generalizations are more or less misleading,' he added.

'Yes, and that includes the one you just made,' replied Master showing an amazing presence of mind.

A general murmur started going on and some even chuckled at Master's sharp jibe.

'Trust me Sir, my intention here is to learn and try to comprehend your policy, which unfortunately my logic suggests is extremely biased. Not only are the statements emanating from the Finance Ministry of the state contradictory but also they're very regressive in nature. The state shows zilch compassion towards labourers who are worst hit by the rising prices. The state goes back on its promised investment in the anti-narcotics initiative, which mind you Sir, you recognized as an absolute necessity in your previous statements,' he continued.

Master's commanding voice backed with a sound rationale was so gripping and insightful that suddenly a vast majority of the students were not only physically attending the session but were also mentally present. He not only pointed out the instances of irregularities in the government's performance but also liberally quoted excerpts from the different annexures of the state and central budgets. Such was the brilliance and purity of his knowledge that it literally became a spectacle.

Mr Vincent Nazareth, on the other end, was absolutely tongue-tied. All that he and other accomplished dignitaries could do was to sit and take notice of a spark that would perhaps one day become an inextinguishable fire. As Master concluded his addressal, he humbly said, 'Sir I know that you must be thinking it's easy for someone to stand here and blabber but difficult to go out there and execute and you're right. But what others and I perhaps want or deserve as citizens is a clear unbiased and an uncluttered communiqué from the Planning Commission and the Finance Ministry at large. Thank you.'

The crowd erupted with applause and all one could hear for a minute were thunderous claps.

Vincent came closer to his mike, looked Master straight in the eye and in a flat yet combustible tone he said, 'That's a point well taken. I would love to answer these questions but perhaps on some other suitable forum. Thank you.'

The students and faculty were sporting enough to clap at Vincent's reply. The dean then whole-heartedly thanked Mr Vincent for his insight and patience. Vincent, however, wasn't really feeling very comfortable and decided to leave after exchanging pleasantries with all. What, however, came to the fore that day was not just Master's honesty towards his subject but also how strongly he felt about certain issues.

It was time to roll up all the books, put aside all the intelligentsia and gear up for the annual college fest 'Geronimo'. This annual fest generally got Goa alive every year. This year it was alive and kickin'. All roads in Goa led to Grinnel's. For three days, hardly anyone in the campus slept. All night one could hear ripples of laughter from some corner or the other.

So charged and high were the people that even the faintest music of some B-grade film was enough to burn the dance floor. The hostel dormitory for those three days was an absolute sight. Messed up tables, torn and used up wrappers and half a dozen empty bottles were stacked in one corner and a slightly larger number of boys were lying wasted in another corner. However, Joseph cleaned up the mess without batting an eyelid or making a fuss. With help from Master he got everything back in order, ensuring that no complaint of indiscipline was lodged against the boys.

The events meanwhile were pompous and the performances by the students and invited artistes were enough to make it a huge spectacle. From speed dating to rock concerts, from fashion shows to the Crystal Maze, Grinnel's was witness to all of it.

The one person who was all over the place was Jack. Now Jack could pull off anything with a reasonable amount of success and charm. The 'Banjara Main' song written in the backyards of the dormitory over a couple of drinks saw the light of the day. Jack sang it with so much depth, fun and ease that leave aside the *surs* and *taals*, people just swayed. It was only a matter of time before 'Banjara Main' became the punchline of the fest.

Master, on the other hand, was the chief coordinator of the event. Master's deep baritone, peppered with a fun yet sophisticated humour gave the event a classy feel. Needless to say the logistics, man management and operations seemed crisp and effortless. Despite all the immaculate management, a minor breakdown happened backstage, bringing things to a screeching halt and delaying the next performance indefinitely.

The full crowd in a mood of revelry and anticipation slowly started getting restless and was waiting for some action.

Master, in a crisis called Jack over and asked him to do something to divert the crowd's attention. Jack didn't really have too many ideas but nevertheless, he spontaneously decided to step in. Jack grabbed a microphone, took to the stage and just spoke off whatever he had at the top of his mind.

'Hello, check...123. Yes, it's working and so is this party. Isn't it?' exclaimed Jack.

Loud shouts of 'Yes' came from all corners.

'You know what guys, for many of us, this might be the last college fest we'll ever be a part of. In fact most of us at this place tonight might never ever see each other in life again. But the point is that if we ever meet, then God dammit, we should look back at this evening and say, "Man we had a kick-ass time. Man that was a moment I want to hold on to forever". Nothing, and I mean nothing stops us from making this moment special,' said Jack in a tone that inhaled oxygen and exhaled pure passion.

'That's right ladies and gentlemen even this minor breakdown backstage can't take this moment away from us. We'll always remember it as that special moment in a happening college fest when a freak, who mind you was very handsome, came on the stage and spoke something straight from the heart,' exclaimed Jack with a smile. The people slowly but surely started connecting with Jack.

'Hey, you know what, the only thing missing in this moment is a performance. Isn't it?' asked Jack.'

'Yes,' was the unanimous reply.

'I mean that's what you guys came here to see, a performance,' said Jack looking through the crowd and then looking backstage. 'Well, then you will have one,' cried out Jack with excitement.

The back stage technicians shouted, 'Hey, we are not ready.'

Jack called out, 'Joseph, can we please have you here?'

Joseph was absolutely surprised to hear his name. He hesitantly smiled and was pretty clueless.

'Come on, Joseph, we want you here...Please,' insisted Jack rather affectionately. Joseph had no idea and though initially hesitant, he gave in to Jack's request and apprehensively walked on to the stage.

Jack introduced Joseph to the people. 'Ladies and gentlemen, give a round of applause for Joseph.'

The crowd clapped and everybody from Master to the backstage crew to Joseph nervously waited to see what Jack was up to. Jack continued, 'Now he has been a part of Grinnel's for the past twenty-five years. He has seen minnows like us dance and sing for a dozen years.' Joseph was all smiles at the attention he was receiving.

'But unlike these dozen years, today he will actually be performing. Do you guys want to see him perform?' asked Jack.

The 'Yes' was so resounding that it literally went through the roof.

'Alright then, Joseph the mike's yours.'

Joseph was smiling hesitantly.

'Come on everybody...Joseph...Joseph...Joseph...' cheered Jack and others followed suit. Master and the organizing team were on tenterhooks to see what really was going to happen.

Five minutes back, Joseph could never have imagined himself standing in the centre of a stage surrounded by hundreds chanting his name. Nervous, excited and above all touched by this gesture, the old man did grab the microphone and then what came out wasn't really the best voice that the crowd had heard, but it sure had a lot of heart.

'My heart is beating. It's all repeating. You make my heart... lalala...'

You bet everyone's heart was beating for this old man. He sang and sang with gay abandon. With a beaming smile across his face and a tear rolling down his eye, the man had the crowd singing with him. Everybody was clapping or laughing.

'For all the 2,500 people out there in Grinnel's that night it was the most special moment of any fest that they had ever been a part of. That is what Jack was. He could conjure a special moment out of a mishap. Phew. But the real suspense of the fest was still waiting,' said Master as the thousand plus attendees at India Gate listened.

After three amazing days, it all came down to the prom night. It was the night where according to Master |a+b| could be greater than |a|+|b| or, in a layman's language, two not so happening individuals could add up and suddenly be the talk of town. Jack had still not received any reply from Samantha. He had been looking at the entrance door all day long.

The prom night was indeed a situation carved out of perfect music, perfect ambience and some not so perfect yet happening couples. It was the sort of place where gossip, rumors and eyebrows were raised, goof ups were dreaded and romance was cherished.

For Jack though it was nothing but pulsating anxiety, 'Will she? Won't she?'

Master tried to comfort Jack but Jack was barely able to comprehend. He did have the consideration to tell Master. 'You've got to propose tonight, okay. And you better do it, before you know, she's like "Uh, I think we need to talk" and you are like "Really?" (imitating Master). Soon she'd be like "You know what, Siddharth, I think there is somebody" and you would be like "Really?" Then she'd be like "Hey, all the best. Thanks for the memories…my wedding is on the 15th of this month" and you'd still be stuck at "Really?" and before you know it, I'd be telling you "Bro, it's been three years. Move on" and you'd still be stuck at that "Really?"'

'Really!' exclaimed Master spontaneously.

'See, exactly,' pointed out Jack.

'Wait, wait. But what about you, ha…why don't you propose?' asked Master.

'She is engaged. Try and understand this. You think I am the kind of guy who sees another man's fiancé and proposes to her. Well, then you are absolutely right,' declared Jack as they high-fived and laughed out loud.

As they were laughing, the gate opened and there entered a woman who completely bowled over everyone not by her stylish outfit or outlandish accessories but by the sheer charm and elegance of her simplicity. Master told Jack, 'That's Sakshi.'

Jack smiled and said, 'Now who says these geeky economists don't get good chicks. Ha…'

Master walked towards Sakshi and with every step towards each other, they could sense a sizzle. It was one of those moments where romance comes etched in purity. Sakshi looked at Master's tuxedo and by her darting eye movement gave it a thumbs up.

Master gracefully caught Sakshi's hand and helped her inside. He blushed and asked her, 'Am I wearing it exactly as you told me over the phone?'

'Oh absolutely, you're a good listener,' she said.

'Know what else I am good at?' asked Master.

'Don't tell me economics,' warned Sakshi.

They both laughed as Master just stepped back, came down

on a knee and asked her out for a dance. Sakshi elegantly extended her hand as the two graced the dance floor. So graceful were they that amongst all other couples wearing pompous clothes and doing extravagant dance steps, they stood out as a simple and fresh couple that didn't really feel the need to make an impact.

Hand in hand, the couple slowly swayed to the tune in their hearts, as Sakshi in her characteristic mischievous demeanour asked Master, 'Siddharth, you didn't tell me how I am looking.'

'Mmmm, you are looking good,' he winked.

'Aha...how good?' she asked, stoking the airs of romance.

The two could barely keep their eyes off each other. 'You're such a kid, Sakshi,' smiled Master.

'I know, but tell me, how good am I looking in the gown?' she insisted.

'Well, the only way I know how to quantify things is by drawing a relatively quantifiable graph,' said Master, the economist.

'Well, then draw one,' she lovingly insisted.

'Are you serious, Sakshi?' smiled Master with surprise.

'Ya...I really want to see those weird graphs you keep drawing,' she said.

'All right then, follow my movements,' Master gently whispered in her ears.

Master's gentle strokes in thin air, began carving out an imaginary graph which only the two could see. The strokes blended perfectly with their dance steps as the two were in a blissful trance.

'You see that door down there, from there right till the drinks counter, we have the y-axis,' informed Master.

'Aha...,' smiled Sakshi. 'What does that represent?' she

asked.

'That's your 'good looks score'. That'll tell how good I think you look in each of your dresses.'

'Can't tell you how excited I am,' smiled Sakshi, holding on to Master's hand.

'And you see that pole at the end of the floor, from there right up till the door, we have the x-axis,' said Master.

'And what's that for?' she excitedly asked.

'Well, that'll have all your amazing dresses which you've been wearing for quite some time,' replied Master.

'Wow...which ones?' asked Sakshi.

'Ah...ah...,' fumbled Master, trying hard to recollect the dresses.

'Say the pink suit I wore on your birthday,' said Sakshi.

'Yes...absolutely,' he said, heaving a sigh of relief. 'Then... ah...ah...'

'How about the orange top that I wore on Christmas?' said Sakshi.

'Fantastic,' replied Master.

'You don't remember, do you?' she asked.

'Now I do,' he sheepishly said.

'You not remembering my dresses really freaks me out, you know that.'

'I know it freaks you out and also, completely pisses you off,' he obediently replied.

Sakshi smiled at Master's innocent jibe to which Master said, 'I love it when you're angry and smiling at the same time.'

Sakshi gently kissed him on his cheek, as he once again started drawing the graph.

'Alright then on x-axis you have my pink suit, my orange top, my high school dress and let's say this white gown that I am wearing,' said a visibly excited Sakshi.

'Absolutely and now here we go,' said Master and just as he was about to draw the next line, something strange happened. All his laughter, all his smiles transformed into a deep introspection or perhaps a realization. Something for sure had struck him deep. He had never felt the way he was feeling at that time. It was something inexplicable, yet very true.

Sakshi was quick to observe this sudden mood swing as she enquired, 'Siddharth, what happened?'

'Nothing. I...I can't do this,' spoke Siddharth in extremely low tones as he suddenly abandoned the graph exercise.

'Okay. But...but, what happened, Siddharth?'

'Sakshi, can we please talk about something else. I mean please,' said Master with a puzzled look.

'Okay,' she said, with a tinge of disappointment and surprise.

After a moment of silence, Master in an attempt to carry on a healthy conversation asked, 'How's your fund raising thing going at the NGO?'

'It's going good,' she replied rather monotonously.

'You mean good as per your expectations or better?' he enquired.

'You want me to draw a graph and explain?' she disgustedly asked.

'Not required,' replied Master.

'No...no...if you want I can draw a graph. Siddharth, that there is the x-axis. Can you see that there?' she mockingly started off.

Master panicked and said, 'Okay, stop. Thanks. Should've known where this was going.'

'What?' she asked.

'Nothing. I think I should get you something to eat and drink,' said Master as he left for the food stall behind.

Jack meanwhile had now reached a point where he just couldn't take the waiting any longer. His exuberance had slowly started giving way to disenchantment. He had been helplessly staring at the door, all evening.

To add to his woes, by now everyone had piled on with someone or the other and that also included Birju and Ankur. Not to mention that this happened after both of them showed their photo-shopped masterpieces to Sneha for whom it was a near death experience.

A disillusioned Jack was sitting at the drinks counter when Master and Sakshi came by to meet him.

'Jack, this is Sakshi and Sakshi, he's Jack,' introduced Master.

'Jack. Yes, I have heard about you,' said Sakshi . 'You are that guy who was chased by a tiger. Right?' she smiled.

'African tiger,' winked Jack. 'Someday, I will tell you the entire story in detail,' he exclaimed.

Sakshi laughed and said, 'Oh, sure, I'll be all ears for that one.'

'Thanks and by the way, you are looking great,' exclaimed Jack.

'Really! How great?' she asked with apparent mischief in her eyes.

'Okay, I'll tell you. In style I'd give you an 8 out of 10. In your looks, you are say eight and a half and in simplicity, oh you rock, it's a perfect 10,' exclaimed Jack.

'Wow! You really illustrated it. Thank God, you didn't need to make a graph,' said Sakshi, looking at Master who was zapped at their complete bizarreness.

'Which idiot draws a graph to answer that?' asked Jack.

'Me,' replied Master with a wry smile.

'Oh, of course, only a super genius like you can do it,' said Jack, biting his tongue. He continued, 'Ah wow, how lucky are you guys, romancing over graphs and all. And look at me sitting here all alone, listening to "I'll be waiting for you".'

'Jack, she won't come. Move on and enjoy the party,' exclaimed Master.

'No, no, Jack, you keep waiting,' suggested Sakshi. 'Girls love to know someone's waiting for them with bated breath and whispering humbleness,' she continued.

'Unlike others,' she sarcastically commented, giving Master a deadpan look.

'Yes, you are right and tell you what, years down the line, even these waiting moments will be memorable,' he fantasized.

Master honestly felt that the two had gone completely bananas. Well, perhaps Sakshi was right and so was Jack because at quarter past nine, the door did open once more and suddenly, Jack could once again hear the trumpets in his mind. The symphony was swelling up and Michael Jackson was singing 'The way you make me feel'.

Jack started moving towards her. He didn't care whether he hit the waiter on his way nor did he bother about getting hit by a dancing couple. Only the binoculars were missing and the rest was deja vu. Jack's world indeed had just turned upside down, yet again.

Somehow, some way Jack did reach Samantha in one complete piece. A smile beamed across his face as he admired Samantha in the Lady Gaga outfit. Yes, everything seemed carved in perfection except for that one flying flick of hair, which Sam very elegantly tucked behind her ear. Jack stood there for a second and then suddenly he freaked out.

'What the hell have you done?'

'What?' asked Samantha in a state of urgency.

'I mean don't you know we have people out here?' asserted Jack.

'What, dammit? What?' shrieked Samantha.

'You have no right to...'

'To what?' she asked.

'To look so freakin', smokin' hot,' chuckled Jack excitedly.

'I mean, amidst so many testosterone-charged homo sapiens, it'd create pandemonium, girl,' said Jack with a smile that wasn't going to fade that evening.

'Well that's the floor and it's calling us, Sam. In fact it just pinged me with a smiley,' he said.

Samantha smiled at Jack's nonsensical jibe and then hesitantly said, 'Jack, I told you, I am not a dancer.'

'Neither am I, but quietly shhh...just listen to me...come.' Jack held her hand and guided her to the floor.

He then passionately whispered, 'Sam, don't see or hear anything. For this moment, absolutely nothing exists in the world, except for you, me and the floor.'

'Ahaa...' she said and then looked into his eyes.

That moment, that shot of Jack and Samantha on the dance floor seemed straight out of a movie scene. There was raw pulsating electricity waiting to light up the floor and then, they danced...

They danced as if there was no tomorrow. Their movements, their dance steps, were following the rhythm of their heart-beats. It sent a thousand hearts racing and perhaps another thousand marveling at the sheer chemistry they shared. Hand in hand, eyes in eyes, the next twenty odd minutes seemed like one moment that flew away on the wings of romance. Their dance was sans any intricate technicalities or heavy duty action, it was an organic extension of the amazing connect they shared. It was not a dance, it was an expression, an expression so aesthetic and graceful that it struck a chord with almost everyone.

And just when everybody thought their dance was all passion, it suddenly took a fun path. As the symphony started swelling up, slowly both Samantha and Jack began clapping and going around. The momentum picked up when all their friends, Master, Sakshi, Ankur and Birju joined together to form a meandering train that danced its way through the entire hall, amidst spills of laughter, excitement, joy and unabashed revelry. It was curtains on what was one fantastic college fest.

Jack and Samantha had by now realized that perhaps they were more than just a great dancing couple.

And as the night started ripening, Jack went to Samantha and said, 'Thanks. I mean, you did come.'

'Yes, it was a fun evening, pretty much like that day,' smiled Samantha.

'I know,' said Jack.

'And we danced…' she exuberantly said. 'Hey you must know, I've always sucked at that,' she said.

'But not anymore, I mean today we had to call the fire department for rescue,' said Jack.

Samantha smiled and asked, 'Could they extinguish it?'

'Some places they could, other places they couldn't,' said an intense Jack.

'Well, then perhaps we shouldn't do this again to avoid trouble, you see,' said Samantha.

'Aha…' exclaimed Jack, as the conversation kept getting more and more intense. Jack came closer to Samantha, held both her hands and said, 'But Sam the thing is, trouble or no trouble, fireman or no fireman, you are the one I want to dance all my dances with.'

Samantha had honestly seen this coming for quite some time and she didn't know how to react. For a moment she didn't say a word, and after thinking hard she nonchalantly replied, 'Look Jack, just so you know, I'm getting married to Aakash very soon.'

'Are you in love with him?' he asked straight up.

'Well, we're getting married so obviously, I must be in love with him,' replied Samantha.

'Must be in love or I am in love?' asked Jack, cheekily fanning the old suspicions that Samantha had.

'Dammit. Don't start off again,' freaked out Samantha as she started walking towards the parking lot on the outside.

'Listen, Aakash is coming over so don't create a scene,' warned Samantha.

'Oh I will not. After all you must be in love with him,' said Jack deliberately stressing the "must be".

Sam kept walking on as Jack from behind shouted, 'Fine but remember one thing. We were sent to planet Earth after an extensive research.'

'What?' asked Sam.

'Yeah right, you see Cupid and his staff had a 3 a.m. round conference and the minutes of the meeting were that in order to salvage the depreciating style quotient of the world, Jack and Samantha would come together as one. You stop this from happening Sam, and you are messing with Mother Nature. You are screwing with Cupid and Cupid...Ha...the guy has a giant ego.'

Absolutely zapped and baffled by what she heard, Sam

said, 'How the hell do you manage to manufacture such a truck load of nonsense, Jack?'

'Well, that's what people told Archimedes, but look what happened. Nobody messes with buoyancy anymore,' replied Jack.

'Oh my God, Jack you have totally lost it. Stop before I also start behaving like you.'

'Hey wait...Aakash is here,' she said.

As Aakash entered Jack discovered something that he could have only feared in his dreams. Aakash was a tall, muscular blue-blooded stud. He was the picture-perfect take-home boy for any girl. Good height, lean body, fat pay packet and a stable job, he was every parents' dream son-in-law and for Jack, he was the Satan of his Cupid-written love story.

Aakash met Jack with a lot of cordiality, but as the conversation got rolling, some interesting things came to the fore.

'Dude, investment banking is the No.1 profession in terms of money as per a *Forbes* report,' said Aakash.

'So you are happy and enjoying your work?' asked Jack.

'It is rated as the No.1 job, so I have to enjoy it,' he confirmed.

'Quite an obvious explanation. So you are the kind of guy, who believes in surveys and polls before choosing,' said Jack.

'Well, that's how it should be. Shouldn't it?'

'Yeah. Is that how you decided to go for Samantha?' remarked Jack cheekily.

Aakash didn't answer for a while but then in a matter of fact way, he said, 'She was selected the head-girl of her college. Everybody I know finds her very beautiful. I mean they'd give her at least an 8 or 8.5 on 10.'

'I'd give her a 12,' stated Jack.

'See, I have my reasons,' said Aakash.

'You sure have them man,' said Jack as he high-fived Aakash. Jack then turned towards Samantha who was attending to someone else she met in the parking lot and he said, 'Sam which agency did you consult to get Aakash?'

Samantha didn't know how to react to this whereas Aakash said, 'What do you mean?'

'I mean, like you had to conduct some research to get her, what did she have,' he mischievously asked.

'Find-my-mister-handsome-banker-husband-dot-com?' Jack said naughtily.

Aakash was quite confused when Jack cleared the air and said, 'Dude that's a compliment to your awesomeness.'

'Tell you what, Jack, you are really weird,' laughed Aakash.

'I know,' said Jack.

'Hey thanks for taking good care of her. You guys had a great time in Goa and a great prom night…Seems you two get along well,' said Aakash.

'Very well actually,' exclaimed Jack. Samantha stared at Jack, but to no avail.

'That's good. Perhaps your likes and your tastes match right,' said Aakash.

'Yeah, she likes really weird,' confirmed Jack.

That statement pretty much nailed it for the day. With these words, Jack left, but not before opening the floodgates to a number of questions.

'Wait a second now, has this guy fallen for you?' asked Aakash.

Samantha quickly went on the defensive and said, 'Look it's not what you think, there's nothing between us, I promise.'

'No…No….tell me, has he fallen for you? Do you think so?' Aakash calmly asked.

'Yes, may be,' said Samantha.

'Yohoo…Yohooo…' Aakash jubilated.

'See, my choice and research proved to be right. You are indeed a boy-killer. Ha…ha…ha and you know what, I'm the lucky boy who'll be killed by you,' laughed Aakash.

Samantha in her royally pissed off tone said, 'I bet you will be.'

.5.

Jacked!

'So, Aakash is one guy who believes in more research than you, Master,' exclaimed Jack.

'Well, I don't mind playing second fiddle to that guy, but I guess someone else does,' replied Master.

'Yeah, that someone else, let's face it, at least had the guts to confess his love,' said Jack, taking a dig at Master.

'Well, I was this close to saying it, you see, but then something, strange happened,' stated Master.

'What?'

'I don't know, but it was something huge that I can't explain,' said Master.

Before they could discuss it any further, the professor of network encryption and security technologies, Mr Bose, entered the class.

'Mr Bose, was an unbelievably short-tempered and arrogant man but the big question really was, what was he arrogant about? The search, I heard was on right from our super seniors' batch,' Master told the gathering at India Gate.

The arrogance of Mr Bose reached a zenith when one day he

said, 'I know myself really well…in fact way too well. I only have one weakness and that is my quest for perfection. I mean, seriously, my perfectionism can actually rattle individuals and there's jealousy, insecurity and a whole lot of negativity which I hate.' Prof Bose never got tired of singing his own praise but just then, Master scoffed at him.

'Sir, what really is perfection? I mean, barring you,' smiled Master.

'Well, Grinnel's IT network under me is another example. Nobody comes close to screwing with it. Our website cannot be hacked.'

'Cannot be?' asked Jack, almost spontaneously.

'You want to say something?' asked the professor.

'Yes Sir, one little thing, the college website that you are talking about…'

'Yes,' asked the professor.

'Sir, I can hack it,' said Jack in a manner as casual as sitting with friends over a coffee. The class laughed a bit, but one cold stare from the professor silenced it in a second.

'Have you been this foolish ever since you entered planet Earth or is it a recently acquired phenomenon?' asked Prof Bose.

'Let me think,' said Jack, as he closed his eyes and tried to figure out something.

The class was trying hard to control its laughter.

'Yes sir,' declared Jack as he opened his eyes.

'What, you've always been this foolish?' confirmed Prof Bose.

'No….no…Sir, I can definitely hack the website. Till now I was thinking "maybe",' said Jack.

'And now?' asked Bose.

'Now I'm 200 per cent sure. In fact, it's not difficult either... Anyone in the class with little cyber knowledge can do it, Sir.'

Jack continued smiling as Prof Bose completely lost control and said, 'You are a donkey who is pretending to be human... Don't do that because donkeys are meant only to carry loads and not run races. Got it?' Prof Bose was at his condescending best.

'Sir, you seem good at identifying donkeys. Looks like, you know them way too well.'

Now the 'way too well', immediately rung a bell with Prof Bose and the entire class, which had earlier heard him stating, 'I know myself way too well.'

The class was in silent splits as Bose got extremely irked and ranted, 'If a $2 student like you hacks this website then I will admit that I am a donkey. Got it!'

Jack just smiled and said, 'All the best, Sir.'

After the class ended, Master gave Jack a piece of his mind. 'Look, you are being a bit too naive here. Abandon the challenge because it's a lose-lose situation for you, either way,' asserted Master.

'I know and that's why I'm going ahead with it,' said Jack.

'Going ahead to lose. Wow are you short-selling in a bearish market,' joked Master in his economics terminology.

'Look, so far in my stay here at Grinnel's I have won a lot of things, great friends, great night outs, fantastic moments, memories and everything. What else do I want to win?' asked Jack romanticizing his stay at Grinnel's.

'So you want to lose things now?' asked Master.

'No, but the fact is that I have nothing else to win. You won't get it. Let it be. Tell me how are things between you and Sakshi.'

'Well indeed, I didn't understand what he meant then, but what happened over the next few days made our eyes pop.'

At midnight, when the students logged on to the college portal to upload their assignments, they didn't see the traditional three spades and heart Grinnel's emblem but what they did see was a gigantic 1024x768 resolution-sized donkey which was hiding its face. On the screen was written 'click here to see my perfectionist face.' A click of the mouse and what everybody saw was a very artistically morphed face of Prof Bose on the donkey's body. The picture changed back to a donkey's face after every few seconds. Then back again to Prof Bose's face. The pendulum between the donkey's face and the professor's face was oscillatingly funny.

The picture said 'I am hacked or should I say I am Jacked'.

The site was so hilarious that in a few minutes it got more than 200 views. However, hilarity actually ensued, when Prof Bose turned up at the college the next day. Everybody who saw him could only picture his morphed donkey face visual.

The professor's walk to the staffroom was similar to the walk of a man who has come out of a swimming pool searching for his clothes. Prof Bose was irate as he met the dean and called for strict disciplinary action. Within no time, the hostel guard was sent over to bring Jack to the staffroom.

Now Joseph, having a soft corner for him tried to drill some sense into him. On their way to the room he told Jack, 'Jack…you are in serious trouble, just don't argue there. Okay. Just apologize…only apologize.'

Joseph hurriedly shot in his last words before entering the room, 'Jack, don't argue at all.'

As Jack entered the room he was surprised to see an entire disciplinary panel seated there. Prof Bose in his characteristic rude tone shredded Jack's character to bits and pieces. Jack, however, didn't lose his cool and said, 'Sir, I had warned you but then you went ahead with the bet.'

The IT personnel, meanwhile, were trying to correct the website.

The dean said, 'Jack, I always thought you were talented.

'And now you think it even more strongly,' smiled Jack.

Prof Bose, losing his control said, 'Shut up…shut up you rascal.' He then turned back and shouted at the IT personnel, 'Dammit, how long will you take to remove this?'

The man hesitatingly said, 'Sir, just stuck at one place.' Jack cheekily offered to help them and said, 'See just use the query table and you will get the encrypted version back.'

'Oh, yes…that was so simple,' said the IT guy.

'That's what I told, Sir but then he didn't listen,' said Jack roasting the professor even more.

'Sir, I am no IT expert, not even close, but honestly sir, your website had kept one huge gap open and that was something I had once read about in my school days and even participated in,' said Jack.

The dean sternly said, 'So were you trying to be this too-big-for-my-shoes over-smart jerk?'

'Sir, I know I crossed a line, but hasn't this also helped us plug the loopholes in our network. Sir, Prof Bose has been humiliating us and our class for quite some time. In fact, for some reason he holds prejudices against specific students. Would you believe that he held couple of them back from giving the exam, not because their work wasn't up to the mark, but because they had argued with him before,' asserted Jack.

'Get lost before I smash your face,' yelled Prof Bose as he charged towards Jack only to be pacified by the others present.

'Jack you have disrespected an esteemed faculty and I want you to apologize immediately,' ordered the dean.

'I do apologize to you for the inconvenience. But, to Prof Bose, I'm not too sure,' stated Jack.

'Well, in that case, I am not left with too many choices, Jack. I give you a day's time. Go back to your room and think about it. Either you offer a written public apology to Prof Bose or you're rusticated,' said the dean. 'Now go, before I lose my cool.'

Jack quietly walked out of the room and headed straight to his dormitory. That entire evening Jack's room resembled a roadside tea spot where every person had an opinion and some advice to offer. After everybody left, Master went up to him and said, 'Jack for what you've done, you owe an apology to Prof Bose, even though he is the biggest empty vessel I have seen.'

Jack gave a pleasant smile and said, 'I know you are right.'

'Thank God, good sense has finally prevailed,' said Master, heaving a sign of relief. Joseph also joined the persuasion bandwagon as Jack calmed them all down and said,

'Fine, I will apologize tomorrow…Now let's forget all this and have some fun tonight,' shouted Jack in an extravagant tone.

'Fun and a party that everybody remembers,' declared Jack to everyone in the dormitory.

What followed was an enjoyable beer bash that ran late into the night or should we say early in the morning.

Everybody danced and sang, except for Master, who was working on a research paper that he had to present at the prestigious Goa Economic Summit the next day. It was supposedly Master's best and most profoundly acknowledged research paper till now.

The next day was a big one for Master and also for Jack, who like any other regular day dressed up, had his breakfast at the college canteen and went straight to the academic section.

From there, he went to the dean's office where the disciplinary committee was awaiting his arrival and apologies. The dean said, 'So Jack, have you made your decision?'

'Oh absolutely, Sir. I was through with it quite fast, I must say.'

'And what conclusion have you reached?' asked the dean.

Jack came forward, shook the dean's hand and said, 'Sir, today is my last day here. Thank you so much for having me here all this while.'

Everyone in the room was taken by surprise. The dean too was bamboozled as he said, 'But you can actually stay here if…'

'What about your degree, your future?' asked the dean.

'Sir, a degree was fourth on my list when I came here.'

'And the first three?' asked the dean.

'First was memories, second was more memories, third was everything else and fourth was a degree. I got a good first three choices. How many people get that?'

'And your future, Jack?' continued the dean.

'Sir, future's something best enjoyed when it's uncertain or may I say insecure, pretty much like our college website under Prof Bose,' winked Jack, taking one final dig at the professor.

Jack then came forward, shook everybody's hand and said, 'Thanks a lot Sir, for everything and if ever we meet again we will remember this meeting as a happy one.'

On this note, Jack met everyone in the faculty room and in the end went to Prof Bose and said, 'Nice meeting you professor, and trust me, I don't hold anything in my heart against you.' With these words, Jack walked out of the dean's office.

The news of Jack's unexpected or rather blitzkrieg reaction spread across the campus. None of them thought it would go this far. Joseph came up to Jack's room where he discovered that all his stuff was packed well in advance.

Joseph asked him, 'So what's next, Jack?'

'Ah…I am loading my stuff in a taxi and going back home to have a nice nap,' he replied.

Joseph stood there and said, 'You know what you are doing, right?'

Jack tried to reply, 'Ah…yeah…I…I…forget it,' he nervously fumbled and hugged Joseph.

There were some heart-felt moments as everybody gathered to say one final goodbye to Jack. Ankur and Birju were perhaps the most emotional of them all.

'Hey we will miss using those choicest of abuses over drinks,' exclaimed Ankur.

'I'm gonna miss you guys but hey, there's nothing to be sad about. We have enough moments to look back and smile always…Phew…we'll keep meeting, don't worry,' he assured them.

'Well Block-B at Grinnel's will always keep an eye out for you,' smiled Ankur.

'Also, keep the quarter ready,' winked Jack.

'My God. I can't believe you're leaving,' cried Birju.

'I'm not…Hey guys don't make this difficult, let's savour

the moment and feel proud of the time, we spent together,' smiled Jack.

'But Jack, before leaving, you have got to tell us one thing,' said Ankur.

Jack nodded and waited for him to speak.

'And I want you to be honest this time.' You could sense by his tone that Ankur was about to ask a rather important question as everybody anxiously waited.

'Who made a better pair with Sneha. Birju or me?'

'Hahahaha...' laughed Jack and the others present. 'Actually guys there's one thing I didn't tell you,' said Jack.

'What?' asked everyone.

'Did I tell you of the time Sneha and I were working on a project?' he mischievously winked.

'Woooo...wooo...,' everybody shouted in anticipation.

'I'm gonna kill you, Jack,' said Ankur.

'Make that "we"', shouted Birju as the two merrily chased Jack outside.

Jack met everyone and bid them good bye. However, one man who was missing was Master.

That was because earlier in the day Master had left for the economic summit to present his research paper on "Corporate Social Responsibility". In layman's terms corporate social responsibility denoted ethical business practices and their contribution to society.

It was early morning when Master, for the first time in his life, entered the Goa District Centre, the venue for the economic summit that year. It was indeed a proud moment and a huge honour for any budding economist to be a part of the Summit. Not to mention the presence of stalwarts and the opportunity to network. Young dynamic minds from around the world gathered there every year and deliberated on key economic issues.

Master was perhaps the youngest of them. He was supposed to present a research paper on an issue which drew diverse opinions. Some considered corporate social responsibility as charity while others saw it as an opportunity to gain credibility and there were others who thought of it as a necessary evil from a profit point of view.

Master had a very fundamental and stoic stand on this. He firmly believed that if credibility is earned, profits will follow. Such was Master's staunch faith that none of his research papers or business proposals ever missed the society aspect of commerce.

Master was sitting quietly at the registration desk for the summit. A middle aged gentleman asked him, 'Do we have to wait here for the registration?' He obviously thought, Master was a volunteer there.

Master politely said, 'Yes sir, you will have to wait here, please have a seat.'

The gentleman sat down and was sorting through some loose papers in his folder when he came across a business card which he carefully read. He then turned to Siddharth and cheerfully said, 'You guys have arranged things really well and it's great to see some young people getting a chance here today.'

Master inquisitively asked, 'Sir, what do you look for in a summit like this?'

The gentleman replied, 'I look for fresh thoughts and perspectives. Honestly though, they are very far and few these days.'

'Today, however, I'm keen on hearing from this (referring to a business card) exciting young fellow,' he said.

'Well, who is he?' asked Master.

'Oh, he's a young student from Grinnel's and his articles have impressed me,' exclaimed the gentleman. Master could barely hold back his smile.

'Must be good?' asked Master, sensing who this boy could possibly be.

'This level of clarity at this age is something rare and special,' said the gentleman.

'Can I get his card?' asked Master.

'Yes, I have one. Here it is.'

'Twenty years later I still have that card kept on my study table.' Thunderous claps echoed through the entire gathering. 'It was the first time, I actually felt that I do perhaps have it in me to be one of those whom I admire.'

But then that confidence was short-lived, as it was Master's turn to present his paper next. After an elaborate introduction and a huge applause, he was welcomed on stage as the youngest speaker of the evening.

Master stood firmly in the centre and pronounced in his deep baritone, 'I have always wanted to be a gardener. A gardener who makes sure all his plants get the right amount of water and manure. A gardener who sows seeds and removes weeds. A gardener who cuts the overgrown branches of a tree to ensure the welfare of the little saplings begging for sunshine. Ladies and gentlemen, this modern day gardener in today's world is an economist. The society is his garden and water and manure are his resources.'

This was the first time Master used this gardener-economist analogy. Years down the line, this analogy became Master's signature style and he even propounded a theory called the Gardener's Dilemma.

However, at that time it didn't really seem like such a great thought to many. The first person who raised his hand and posed a question to Master was the same gentleman who had met him at the registration counter.

The man was pleasantly surprised to see Master there as he asked him, 'Isn't corporate social responsibility nothing more than an erosion of economic value in the name of charity?'

Loud cheering meant there were many who seconded the gentleman's opinion. 'My counter question to that is, isn't taxation an erosion of people's money in the name of development,' came Master's prompt reply.

His sharp remark met with a lot of reactions from all corners of the gathering. Some just laughed, some even clapped, others called it naive and some just smiled and admired the young man's sharp off the feet thinking. However, certain sections got more vocal and claimed that development is vital. Master further elaborated his stand saying, 'Development is not just the terrain of those who are educated and working hard, but it's also for those who want to be educated, who want to work hard and be a valuable asset, but can't because of lack of resources, because they didn't have the guidance that perhaps you and I were blessed to have.' Master's blending of societal concern along with economic rationale was top-notch as his addressal continued.

'Now, as a budding economist I do realize that profit maximization and value creation for shareholders is your primary objective. And, that's exactly what I suggest here today.

We need taxes for development, as you all rightly pointed out. I say let's raise the number of tax payers in the country. Invest in the higher education of those who need it and empower them to earn a high living and pay taxes.' Master was on a roll.

'You say that we need cost-cutting techniques, cheap labour etc. I say let's do that. Invest in their skill-building and then sign under-priced agreements for their services.' Master gave meaningful suggestion after suggestion. After a long time, economists had heard someone echo the sentiments of welfare economics, a branch popularized by Nobel laureate Amartya Sen.

After the summit, Master left for Grinnel's, curious to know about Jack's fate in the college.

After he reached the hostel, Joseph told him about the turn of events and how Jack wanted to meet Master before leaving but couldn't. However, Jack had left a mark on not just everyone's mind but also on the B-block hostel wall on which he had written "Jack and Master were here" in bold calligraphy.

'Indeed, we were there and that will perhaps be the place where we spent the best times of our lives, but then it was time for us to move on and face the music,' said Master. 'I was pissed off with Jack and wanted to give him a piece of my mind, but that job was quite nicely being executed by someone else.'

'What the hell were you thinking?' shouted Samantha over the webcam.

'About you,' replied Jack promptly.

'That's not funny.'

'Oh yes, only investment bankers are funny, right?'

'Jack, what's the matter?' asked Samantha rather seriously.

'Nothing, I don't know. I just did what felt right, you know. That's how I've always been,' said Jack, scratching his head and looking slightly lost.

'But that's not how life works. If you don't plan things here, this world will eat you up,' she warned.

'Well, then all I say to the world is, bring it on, let's see who eats whom,' said an optimistic Jack in his characteristic style.

The optimism, however, faded in a few seconds. After a brief moment of silence he continued, 'I am not so confident, honestly. In fact, deep down, I get this churning feeling of late but hey, I'm cool with that because that's the fun.'

'Strange kind of fun you enjoy,' said Samantha.

'Hey, why don't you come down, I really want to meet you,' said Jack.

'Nope, I have got to put the wedding plans on track. By the way, we are getting married on the 26th of February,' replied Samantha.

A shadow passed over Jack's face. It struck him like a thunderbolt and for a moment he stayed absolutely quiet.

Regaining his composure he said, 'That's quite quick. I mean nice, congratulations.'

'Yeah thanks. You will come, right?' asked Samantha.

'Oh, of course…of course. I mean, why won't I? I'm unemployed, idle, looking for food and music to dance to. I will come,' said Jack as he freaked out a bit.

'Jack, are you okay?' asked Samantha.

'Oh, I am so very okay. In fact I've never been so okay. I mean my future is bright and sunny, I have girlfriends to choose from, a laptop to video chat on and above all, I have the very well-researched, take-me-home, I'm-so-marriageable, investment banker Aakash on my friend list. Can you beat that?' said Jack.

Samantha laughed out loud and said, 'You are so clearly freaked out.'

'No, I'm not,' denied Jack.

'Yes, you are.'

'No, I am not,' reiterated Jack.

'Yes, you are,' enunciated Samantha.

'Yes, I am,' admitted Jack as Samantha laughed her lungs out.

'But then it doesn't matter to you. I mean, you'll still marry him, won't you?' asked Jack.

'Of course I will,' she replied.

'Dammit,' cried out Jack.

'What? Were you expecting me to say no? Grow up Jack,' laughed Samantha.

Jack smiled and said, 'I really wish I had met you before Aakash. Don't you wish the same?'

There came a brief moment of silence.

'And this time I am not expecting you to say "No",' the words came straight from his heart.

It actually made Samantha think and there was a long pause which was broken by Jack's ringing phone.

'Think about the answer Samantha. I have got to take the call.'

༄

'That call was the first of around five hundred calls including mine, that Jack received that week,' exclaimed Master.

'The Goa Times had posted an article about a university

whiz-kid who had pulverized Grinnel's into submission. Such was the reception and gossip surrounding this news, that Jack's phone just didn't stop ringing that weekend,' laughed Master.

The crowd at India Gate couldn't stop smiling and were waiting to hear more.

Jack, meanwhile, had now started contemplating offers he was getting from different companies who needed professional hackers and web experts. He was apprehensive about taking up something, because he knew he wasn't remotely close to being an expert. Moreover, Jack didn't really consider hacking as a very ethical thing to do.

Nevertheless, weeks later, Jack instinctively accepted an offer from the Goa Web Security Department where besides constructive hacking his job involved sharing the insights and perspectives of potential hackers. That was quite a leap for a college drop-out.

.6.

It Was a Straight Line!

Talking about leaps, there was another gentleman who by now wanted to take a big leap in his relationship but something kept holding him back.

'Sakshi do you really like someone stating what is obvious?' asked Master, stressing "obvious".

'Obvious as in the typical it-rains-in-Goa-in-June obvious or the not so typical hey-I-am-with-you-every-day-so-some-five-thousand-two-hundred-and-sixty-three-days-later-also-I'll-still-be-with-you obvious?'

'What kind of obvious?' Sakshi asked.

'Wow, that's really critical analysis,' said Master.

'Can't blame me, I usually hang around with an economist,' she smiled.

'Assuming the latter,' said Master.

'The not-so-obvious one?' she confirmed.

'Yes,' nodded Master.

'Well, if it ain't completely obvious then it ain't obvious at all,' she said categorically.

Sakshi's statement stunned Master and he slipped into introspection.

'Aha, you are right. It's just that some guys don't state the obvious. It's difficult for them,' said Master, in a disappointed-with-self tone.

He continued, 'Anyway, just a couple of months more and then we have graduation night. The party will run late into the night so I guess you can stay over at my place.'

'Why do you think I'll attend the party?' asked Sakshi.

'Come on, it's obvious,' said Master.

'Well, I don't think so,' came her rather cold reply as she walked out of the room.

Master wasn't expecting this. One thing that became very clear was that obvious or not-so-obvious, Master had to express his feelings for Sakshi.

However, what kept him occupied over the next few weeks were his final post-graduation exams and placements. There was never a doubt in anybody's mind about the fact that Master would walk away with the best placement from the batch. In fact, Master already had multiple offers in his kitty. But then, as they say, no great path is a conventional one. Master surprised everybody by withdrawing his name from the placement process. He turned down some heavy pay packets and mouth-watering designations. The students and faculty both were surprised by his decision but they were all pretty sure that he had something up his sleeve. It all opened up on graduation night.

'Graduation night was one of the most defining nights of my life for three reasons. I will tell you about them one by one...' Master continued.

Reason one.

The convocation ceremony at Grinnel's was always a high profile one. That year, the head of the state planning commission was invited to confer the degrees.

A huge party was waiting to erupt right after the function. With the final exams behind them Master anxiously awaited the result. After a series of awards, prizes and conferment of degrees, it all came down to the coveted "Student of the Year" award.

The Planning Commission Head came to the podium and declared, 'The student of the year and the gold medalist of this batch on the basis of grades and unanimous choice is Siddharth Rane.'

Everybody jumped with joy and excitement. There was not a single person who didn't know the outcome. They were just waiting to hear it officially.

Master sighed and smiled in contentment. He looked through the crowd and all he could see were happy faces reveling in his success. Joseph was clapping the loudest. Master walked to the podium with dignified composure. After exchanging pleasantries with everyone he took the stage and addressed the crowd.

Reason two.

He said, 'I am a trained gardener today.' The crowd instantly connected with the garden analogy, which had by now become famous among the students, as they laughed and clapped whole heartedly.

'You know guys the best thing about being a gardener is that he is never confined to just one garden. He is independent and is employable not to a garden but to the cause of gardening. I wish to be the same and that's why, I have decided not to take up any job but start my own independent consultancy.'

The crowd cheered for Master and wished him luck as Master continued his addressal with renewed passion.

'Today, standing here with you I can proudly say that there was not a single day when I didn't go to bed in the night and thank God for such an amazing day.' The crowd was glued to Master's speech which swayed between nostalgia and optimism.

'The seed sown two years back is a blossoming flower today and with God as my witness, it shall be a ripened fruit tomorrow.'

The entire student gallery was going through a plethora of emotions. Master was in a different zone as he continued, 'The transition that we are going through today will perhaps define how green the garden of our life will be, how tall the tree of our success will be and how firm and solid our roots are. Thank you and God bless us all.'

With these words Master took a bow in front of an emotionally charged crowd which had never in two years shied in giving him a thunderous reception. Such was the weight of Master's words that years later, even today, that speech continues to receive a record number of online hits.

Reason three
Having made the big decision of going independent with his own consultancy, it perhaps was time for Master to take another big decision.

Right after the graduation party he drove straight to Sakshi's home.

∽

'It was one of those days when I just knew that I had to cross

all the 't's and dot all the 'i's. Nothing would have stopped me that night.'

Siddharth was extremely disturbed by the fact that Sakshi hadn't come for his big moment. He went to her apartment but found it locked. As he turned back and walked down the stairs, he felt there was a deep void bothering him. Call it a mix of emotions, or the need to express his feelings at that time, at that moment Siddharth broke down. While walking past the apartment he saw Sakshi standing right in front of him. There was pin drop silence as a vulnerable teary-eyed Siddharth walked towards Sakshi.

He looked her in the eye and said, 'You want to know what graph I wanted to draw on prom night?' He could hardly hold back his tears as Sakshi also felt something moist down her cheeks.

'What did you want to draw?' asked Sakshi.

Siddharth came closer to Sakshi, held her hand and said, 'I saw you for the first time in the third standard when you came to our school. You were wearing that tiny blue skirt and a red baby scarf. You remember that?'

'I…don't remember,' she said.

'Well, I do and also your Popeye the Sailor tiffin box.'

'Oh yes, I loved that. You remember that?' said Sakshi with astonishment.

'I also remember the green dress you wore at the primary school fancy dress and the frock that you wore on New Year's Day when you came to my house for the first time.'

'Oh my God, am I dreaming? Siddharth Rane remembers all my clothes? This is like my happiest day ever. You are such a darling!' she exclaimed, pulling his cheek.

'I know. What I also realized on prom night was that the only graph that could be drawn between what you wear and how beautiful you look is a single straight line.'

Siddharth's voice kept getting heavier with every word and every dropping tear.

'Oh my God,' exclaimed Sakshi as she seemed to absorb the depth of his words. But the very next moment she said, 'I didn't get you. For God's sake make it simpler.'

'Okay, I will, I will. That night at the prom party, I realized that whether you wear those tiny baby pants, the blue skirt or the golden gown, for me you are the most beautiful woman in the world and that's beyond the dresses you wear, beyond the cosmetics you use. I love you, Sakshi,' said Siddharth as his hands trembled with emotion.

'Oh my God, Siddharth,' Sakshi affectionately curled her arms around his neck. 'I never knew a simple straight line could say so much.'

'This simple straight line can possibly be the only tangent to the curve of my life and of all the facts and theories that I have studied in my career, this shall be the one hypothesis I want to spend the rest of my life with.' The intensity of Siddharth's words was such that he broke down. After composing himself he bent down on one knee, picked up his trophy in his hand and said, 'Sakshi will you...will you marry me?'

For a moment all that could be heard was their pulsating heart-beats as Sakshi said the magic word 'Yes'. The two hugged each other. The tears didn't stop, the breaths didn't slow down. So charged were they emotionally that for a good five minutes, they didn't speak a word or move an inch.

Siddharth said, 'I love you. I love you ever since I can

remember and I thought it was obvious.'

'Trust me, it was not so obvious,' exclaimed Sakshi.

Siddharth wiped Sakshi's tears and kissed her on her forehead as she said, 'But you know what is obvious? Obvious is that I would never in the world miss you achieving something that you wanted.'

'Yes, but I wish you were there,' said Siddharth, with a tinge of disappointment.

Sakshi held his hands affectionately and said, 'Honey, when you won that trophy today and walked down the stage, there was one woman standing in the crowd, silently clapping and absorbing the moment. I would not miss it for anything in the world,' said Sakshi.

Siddharth kissed Sakshi on her hand, as the two gently hugged each other. Sakshi said, 'Everything about the occasion today was perfectly well-matched except for one thing.'

'What?' asked Siddharth.

'Your damn tie. I mean it's the biggest moment of your life and you are wearing a golden tie with a black suit,' said Sakshi.

The people at India Gate chuckled with laughter. Master too laughed and said, 'Twenty years later, ladies and gentlemen, I have managed to make the same mistake.'

The crowd was in splits as they looked towards Sakshi, sitting quietly with her eight-year-old son. Graceful as ever, she responded with a warm smile.

'Twenty years, and her smile is still for me the best sight there is on God's green earth.'

So overwhelming were Master's words that Sakshi couldn't stop blushing. The crowd clapped and one or two mischievous ones even whistled in fun.

'What happened next, Sir?' asked one of the inquisitive ones from the crowd.

'Well, I guess after you say "I want to marry you" you better actually marry her,' remarked Master in his characteristic deadpan style.

'I bet, you are thinking that's way too conventional, right?' he asked with a beaming smile across his face.

'Well, trust me that day was everything but conventional.'

.7.

And Then Began the Tough Part

A quiet Goan evening was host to the wedding of Mr and Mrs Rane's son Siddharth with Sakshi. Everything, from the decoration to the arrangements, was simple and graceful, pretty much like the couple.

However, there were two men named Birju and Ankur who had such a God-gifted knack of pedestrian dancing that they could make any occasion look flashy and cheesy. In fact, they had even prepared a performance on a medley of songs. So enthused and yet so loving were they that Master did not have the heart to stop them.

Master's wedding was a Grinnel's reunion of sorts. Almost all of his friends were there except for one gentleman who also, was attending a wedding that very day.

The only difference was that this wedding was far more extravagant. The arrangements were as lavish as the pay-scale of an investment banker and everything from the colour of the curtains to the type of cushions was well researched. It was way too perfect and way too meticulous for a feisty fun loving girl who loved Lady Gaga gowns and adventurous races.

Yes, Jack was there. Even though till five hours ago, he was getting ready in a different city to attend a different wedding. All said and done, he was there and headed straight to meet Samantha.

Samantha in her wedding gown looked so gorgeous that evening that the pompous decorations and glitters around seemed mere pop-ups and add-ons. As Jack entered her room behind the main wedding stage, there was a strange awkwardness between the two. They both looked at each other and then suddenly Jack broke the ice by saying, 'What are you doing? I mean, you know it's not right?'

Samantha's friends and relatives were appalled and puzzled at Jack's words. Samantha, however laughed loudly to hide her disgust, 'Yeah right, hahaha. And how's everything?'

Something struck Jack as he clapped his hands a couple of times and then after grabbing everyone's attention said, 'Everyone…Hi! I'm Jack. I have a decent paying job, a small decent flat and, needless to say, I'm quite handsome.'

A general murmur started in the room.

'So, the fact is, what is happening here is not right. I mean, this girl here is not at all interested in bonds, debentures, investments and research. She is way too chilled out for all this and hey guess what, so am I. So, what should be happening here is this (pointing to Samantha and himself) rather than this (pointing to Samantha and a distant Aakash). And you know what, I am pretty sure you all will be very sporting.' Jack smiled as he nervously rattled off all that was on his mind.

For two minutes nobody moved, no one even blinked. Samantha's jaw remained gravity-bound for some time. Jack grabbed some chips from a serving bowl and while munching on them he said, 'That sounded slower and more gradual in my head, but now that I've said it, please make it quick because otherwise with everyone coming, it'll get very complicated.'

'And right now, it's all very simple,' freaked Samantha. Some of her relatives got irate and charged towards Jack.

Samantha, however, intervened, 'Relax everyone. I will handle this. Everything is fine and normal. Trust me.'

Samantha shouted at Jack and said, 'What in blue hell are you doing here?'

Aakash by now had heard the story and he came rushing to the green room. He looked Jack in the eye and before he could do or utter anything, Jack embraced him tightly and kissed him. 'I love you, man. You are a stud and you know it,' piped Jack.

The situation was getting so hysterical that it was hard to believe it was happening for real. Aakash quickly broke out of Jack's embrace and fuming with rage he said, 'Back off Jack, before you're dead.'

'Listen Aakash, I don't like what I'm doing but hey, you guys aren't I-love-you-and-want-to-spend-my-life-with-you. You guys are Okay-she's-pretty, tick, He's-well-settled, tick, She's-a-prize-catch, tick,' pointed out Jack.

'I will kick your…,' Aakash said furiously.

'Butt and that too very badly, I know. But hey, Aakash, trust me, brother, this marriage isn't good for anyone. It's like the partition of 1947 which didn't serve any purpose?'

'Enough. Time to shut you up,' yelled Aakash as he ambushed Jack.

Samantha, however, came forward and tried to pacify Aakash and then went straight to Jack.

'Jack, listen, this is my wedding and I do not need you here,' she stated.

'Then where exactly do you need me?' asked Jack.

'What business do you have being here and creating a ruckus?' asked Samantha.

'Business? No, no, I don't have a business to run or take

care of. Investment bankers do. Not me,' piped Jack.

Aakash was getting angry at the banter and was ready to attack Jack. However, others stopped him as Samantha pushed Jack outside and dragged him till the main gate.

'Now will you please leave this place,' she shouted.

'Look, I love you from the moment I saw you. Even after that, if you want me to leave I will,' said Jack.

Jack went out of the gate and walked to his car. And just when everything seemed under control Samantha shouted, 'Yes you better leave.'

'I wonder, what else I am doing,' remarked Jack.

'Yes, you should leave. You have no business here,' shouted Samantha.

'You leave and I will never be able to...,' sighed Samantha.

'Able to?' asked Jack.

'Able to see you. I will never be able to see you,' realized Samantha.

'You think you can get away from this place?' she angrily asked.

'Sure. I mean who can stop me?' asked Jack.

'There are three guards from here till the main gate. You think you are smart enough to beat every one and run away?' she shouted.

'Hell yes!' Jack shouted back.

'Then what are you waiting for? Open the damn door,' yelled Samantha.

Before anyone could gauge the awkwardness of the moment Samantha slipped into Jack's car, took a couple of deep breaths and shouted, 'Run, Jack, run.'

So hysterical was the situation that they didn't know whether to laugh, be serious or act. Aakash, his parents,

Samantha's parents, everyone turned into sitting ducks as Jack smiled and said, 'Nobody's catching me, sweetie.'

He reversed his car a decent distance and then effortlessly zigzagged his way out, deceiving everyone on the way. It pretty much symbolized Jack's journey with Samantha as these two eloped with each other rather instinctively.

'What are we doing, Jack?' asked Samantha.

'Well, that's what people call eloping,' explained Jack laughing out loud.

'I never thought I would do such a thing in my life,' said Samantha.

'Well, welcome to my part of the world,' winked Jack. He paused for a second and then corrected himself. 'In fact, our part of the world.'

'Oh yes, the two got married on the same night that Sakshi and I got married, the only difference being that ours was a lot more planned and organized,' stated Master.

People laughed and listened with keen interest as Master continued, 'And then began the tough part of our lives...'

It was the early days of Masters' Consultancy Pvt. Ltd. Even though Master's academic credentials were a big lure, corporates did not immediately put their money on a beginner. However, he kept his patience and worked tirelessly to promote his idea of a free market system where labour laws and wages were better defined and fair. He wrote journals and articles for leading economic papers and magazines.

Master's popularity kept rising as he started receiving

invitations to speak across different forums, conferences and summits. These networking opportunities did help him build a small client base. However, a strong majority of corporate houses were still averse to Master's policies. Nevertheless, his natural flair towards welfare economics helped in creating a very distinct and unique image in the minds of the people. Little did anyone know that this flair would one day assume proportions that no one could ever have fathomed.

Talking about proportions that no one could have ever fathomed,' Jack also wasn't very good at fathoming things in advance.

The net security job, though interesting, was perhaps more than Jack could chew.

However, Jack was smart enough to pull off his work reasonably well. He was unconventional yet decently effective. One day his boss, the security chief, sat down with him and asked him, 'Jack, why do you think someone just hacks a network and then leaves without doing anything?'

'Sir, hacking is often just an ego drive,' exclaimed Jack.

'I mean it's like winning the attention of that hot girl who you might want to date, but never really marry and start a family with,' laughed Jack.

'Okay, so guess who your next chick is…,' he said.

'Hope it's not one of those smoking hot, hard as nuts bimbos,' exclaimed Jack.

'Well, it is a telecom giant. Hacking their network can get us some crucial inputs,' expressed the boss.

'Well, that isn't going to be a walk in the park,' said Jack.

Jack's boss laughed and said, 'Take your time. I am sure you'll have her weak in the knees pretty soon.'

Finishing his drink he asked, 'And by the way how is life

post marriage?'

'Oh, life after marriage? Well, that's the stuff heaven's made of, Sir. You see, I'm the man of the house who works hard and after a long day's work is welcomed home with a beaming smile from a doting wife who never tires of inquiring about my fatigue. She is so concerned and bothered that she serves me hot food which she cooks herself and then she tenderly says "I love you darling".'

'Oh my God, Jack. Is everything okay?' asked his boss.

'Oh absolutely,' replied Jack. Jack's boss left and after a while Jack also left for his heaven-like home.

The man of the house did come home and was welcomed by a volley of queries, not about his fatigue but about why he didn't call her or why he did not come for her fashion launch party.

'Darling, I am so hungry,' said Jack in a rather sweet way.

With a beaming smile and an even more sugar-coated tone, Samantha said, 'Honey, I am too disgusted with you.'

'Oh yes, you know what? I love you,' said Jack with a hope of normalizing things.

'Sweetie, that won't work with me anymore,' she smiled.

'All right, it was my mistake, I am sorry,' said Jack.

'You just want to get things back to normal, right?' said Samantha.

'Of course, I do,' he replied.

'Dammit! You aren't really sorry, are you?' exclaimed Samantha.

'No. I mean, yes. I mean what should be the right answer here?' asked a bamboozled Jack.

'You are such a…uhhhhh,' said an irritated Samantha.

'Such a sweetheart,' said Jack, completing the sentence.

Samantha looked away in disgust. Jack said, 'Sam, I got late with this damn encryption-decryption shit. They all want me to get some key, some password and God knows what all.'

'There were models, there were designers. So much glamour and fun…,' said Samantha.

'And then, they asked me how do you really find the key to this code.'

'There were some really nice dresses too, by the way.'

'I said the key to anything is either something random or way too intrinsic to that anything.'

'I wore a red gown and everyone, even that jealous bitch Sarika, complimented me.'

'For example, if you are looking for a key to my happiness then there can be only one name written on it and that's Samantha.'

'The only thing missing there was your presence. All the compliments mean so little in front of your single smile of assurance,' Samantha said with moist eyes.

'I love you and you know that,' said Jack.

'I know,' said Samantha, as they both hugged each other.

Jack and Samantha were one crazy couple. One could never know when they would be at loggerheads and when they would be sugar and honey.

∽

However, one person who wasn't sweet and honey for the corporate giants of Goa was Master. He had lambasted many business models which offered little scope for societal development. Master's consultancy hadn't quite picked up huge momentum and all they had were a handful of Small to Medium sized Businesses (SMBs) and a couple of startup ventures as clients. The man was itching to make an impact at a macro level but the corporate giants still didn't buy his ideas.

Months passed and there were times when it all looked gloomy and bleak. In his restless times, Master would just switch off and go visit Sakshi's NGO. Little children with hopes in their eyes and aspirations in their hearts were always a pleasant change for Master.

It was on one such day that Master got slightly philosophical and said, 'You know Sakshi, these kids are taught in school that nothing is impossible. Go out there and live your dream. But that isn't the truth, is it?'

'Siddharth, what happened?' asked a slightly worried Sakshi.

'Nothing. I mean, all my life I've wanted to be an independent economist who could bring a change, who could make helping kids like these a responsibility rather than a charity. But here all I have are hopes and dreams and nothing concrete,' expressed Master. One could literally sense that Master was slowly but gradually breaking down from inside.

Sakshi kept her hand on Master's folded palms and said, 'Siddharth, look at me, honey. I do not have the slightest doubt that you will succeed.'

'Really,' said Siddharth in a husky tone which exuded uncertainty and indecisiveness.

'Oh you will. Trust me, I know it. It's destined that you will be the best at what you do,' said Sakshi as she warmly cuddled him.

In a very low and barely audible tone, Master said, 'You know Sakshi, you are my inspiration. When I see you doing what you do, I feel so small. I wish I could do something of this sort, in my way.'

'You haven't chosen an easy path, Siddharth,' she said. 'But if there is anyone who can tread on it with dignity and grace, it's you. People just go about criticizing policies, blaming it on systems and administration but you have gone out there and taken the bull by its horns,' emphasized Sakshi.

'Whatever happens, I am proud of you,' smiled Sakshi, as she affectionately patted his cheek.

'Well, as long as you're proud of me, I cannot fail. I just cannot,' he said gently kissing her hand.

Master's voice got heavier as he spoke and for the first time one realized that behind this man of stoic resolve and nerves of steel was a human. A human perturbed at uncertainty, scared at the prospect of darkness and relieved after a word of assurance.

'So, Mr all-grown-up-yet-so-kiddish economist,' repeat after me, 'Nothing is impossible.'

'Nothing is impossible,' reiterated Master, rather obediently like a child.

'Go out there and live your dream,' said Sakshi.

'Go out and live your dream,' enunciated Master as a pleasant smile slowly spread across his face. He affectionately kissed her forehead and went back to his study.

No miracles happened after that night. Master's struggle continued for years together, the only difference being that Master was now learning to live with it.

The other man who was learning to live with all this security-insecurity mumbo-jumbo was the chief consultant of web security. He wasn't very gung-ho about the telecom assignment he had recently received. One, it was notches above anything that Jack had even attempted and secondly, Jack didn't really like the idea of getting into someone's living room and listening to what was none of his business. Anyway, it was the quarterly bash thrown at Grenade's Hotel where Jack and his team members were having a ball.

Samantha accompanied Jack for what was a kick-ass party, pretty uncharacteristic, considering it was mainly for techno geeks and uptight security officials.

Rehan, one of Jack's peers at work, introduced Samantha to Jack's boss, Mr Nair, and the others present at the party. Jack meanwhile was completely in his mould that night. Partying and wining to glory, he was having a ball.

Mr Nair came over and raised a toast in the name of Jack and Samantha who were also celebrating their first wedding anniversary that night. The crowd cheered and happily greeted the couple.

Mr Nair said, 'Enjoy the party Jack, and I have a nice anniversary gift for you which I'll announce later in the night. Till then let's all get drunk and lost.'

Samantha was very excited and happy at all the attention meted out to her and Jack. Jack came to her with a drink in his hand and said, 'I suck at making decisions but sweetie, a year back I made the best decision of my life.'

Samantha smiled and caressing his hair lovingly she said, 'I know, honey.'

Jack replied, 'How can you say you know, you were all apprehensive when I told you. Remember?' 'Yeah, but then I also realized,' she said.

'And it all happened by accident,' claimed Jack.

'Call it accident or chance,' replied Samantha as she affectionately cuddled him.

'Had it not been for Prof Bose challenging me to hack his site, this would never have happened.'

The statement rang a bell in Samantha's mind and she quietly asked, 'Jack, what decision are you talking about?'

'Honey, I am obviously talking about my decision of taking this job at Web Security Intelligence,' he replied.

'Oh my God, I have been such a fool, oh my God,' panicked Samantha.

'No, no you're not a fool. Trust me. I mean yeah, one or two instances, here and there aside, you are not a fool,' assured Jack.

Samantha was so furious that she just shrugged off Jack's arm around her shoulder and walked towards the drinks counter. Jack didn't realize what had really upset her, but then a couple of moments later, the bulb did light up.

'Oh my God,' he shouted and before he could make it to Samantha, every one hugged him and danced merrily around him.

These oh-my-God moments were by now a common occurrence in Jack and Samantha's life. Nevertheless, the party kept getting louder and wackier. Jack went up to Rehan and said, 'Where is Samantha? Have you seen her somewhere?'

'Why? What did you do?' he asked.

'Nothing, man. Just a husband-wife thing. You'll never understand,' said Jack.

'It'll be okay. Hey, you know what, I just got to know the big news Nair's announcing tonight,' said Rehan.

'What?' asked Jack.

'You remember our project head, Steve?' asked Rehan.

'Yes, that bugger left…wait…wait…You mean to say, you're the next project head. Give me a high five on that,' said Jack, raising his palm.

Rehan said, 'The only difference is that you are the new project head.'

Jack's jaw dropped to that. 'What are you saying? I mean, are you serious?' he exclaimed.

Rehan hugged Jack and congratulated him. Any normal man would have been on top of the world for getting such a quick promotion, but then Jack and normal didn't go hand in hand. He was completely out of sorts for the rest of the evening. However, Samantha came to him later and just when Jack was about to offer his apologies, she stopped him and said, 'No need honey. Rehan just told me about your promotion and I'm so happy.'

She hugged Jack and said, 'I don't want to be a spoil-sport and fight with you today. I know you love your job and it's great that you are doing well here.'

Jack stopped her and said, 'But I am not. I did love my job but do I still love it. Do I still feel the need to get up from my bed and hack into people's personal space? I don't know.'

'Stop it honey. Very soon you'll be the state head, then the country head, then God knows what,' said a dreamy and relatively satisfied Samantha.

Jack smiled at her and just hugged her without saying anything else. 'I just want to tell you that a year back I made a decision which kicked the butt of all the decisions I ever made in my life.'

'You better be on target this time Jack.'

Jack nodded, smiled and said, 'And that decision was to go to your wedding, cheat the shit out of all your relatives and your investment banker fiancé and elope with a fairy like you.'

'Yeah, we made them look like losers,' exclaimed Sam,

remembering that moment.

'Haha, I still remember their faces. God, they were sore losers,' teased Jack as the two of them laughed to glory.

As the night progressed, everybody eagerly waited for Mr Nair to come and make the important announcement. Samantha happily waited for the announcement. But just then Jack clapped his hands and drew the crowd's attention towards himself. He jumped on to the table and said, 'You all are the most amazing people.'

'You know, around a year back when I joined you I thought I won't be able to hang around for long. I am not that good.'

The crowd nodded in disagreement. He, however, didn't agree and said, 'Oh trust me, pulling this far hasn't been a walk in the park for me. I am not an expert or a degree holder. But today, I just want to make one announcement.'

Glued to Jack's words, everybody was on tenterhooks waiting to hear further.

'And that is, that as an employee of Web Security and Intelligence Department, Goa, today is my last day.'

Everybody looked in disbelief and some even dismissed it as a spillover after alcohol. However, Jack was quick to respond, 'Those who think I'm drunk have no idea of what a tanker I am. Trust me, I'm just getting started.'

Samantha was livid and so were many others. Mr Nair, Rehan, nobody could believe their ears. Nair asked him whether a better offer from some private company was the reason.

However, Jack just quashed all these speculations and said, 'Guys, I don't have a job in my hand. I didn't even apply for one. And Mr Nair, you've been a sweetheart. I don't have any complaints. Why am I leaving? What am I going to do tomorrow? I don't really know. It's just that I think that's it. Me and hacking were only meant to be till here.'

The wanderer in Jack was beginning to reflect but then he brushed all thoughts aside and said, 'But what I do know is that this moment with you all is special. And yes, one final request guys, please don't ask me any more questions. Just enjoy the moment with me and let's make this moment count.'

However, one person who didn't buy this live-the-moment cacophony was his wife. She didn't say anything and walked off. Jack tried to stop her, but in vain.

That was Jack's first marriage anniversary. However, in another part of Goa there was a quiet get together to celebrate another marriage anniversary. No hullabaloo, no lavish party, nothing but a hope to see better times. Master by now realized the need to build some awareness about his opinions and beliefs about welfare economics. He realized that corporate houses won't accept it unless there is a rock-solid positive word of mouth. He had to knock on the door both hard and long enough to get somewhere.

In a bid to effectively market his thoughts and ideas, Master liberally accepted offers to speak his mind across every conceivable forum. Over the course of the next five months, Master toured across the length and breadth of not just Goa, but many major parts of central India, some pockets of north India and even a few strategic places in the South.

'I never used to buy the Bhagwad Gita logic that you must work hard and not worry about the result. But trust me, as years pass by you realize that this is indeed the single biggest reality

of our life. Accept it now or realize it later, it's your call,' said Master as his journey continued to unravel.

⤴

Months and months passed by but Master hadn't received a single concrete order. However, it all seemed to change one day. It was just any other morning for Master until the phone rang. Master's office secretary picked up the phone and the call was from Boyd and Co. It was a retail giant having their headquarters in Mumbai and a key branch office in Goa. They had some firm consolidation plans and wanted to see Master on the same.

A determined yet nervously excited Master entered the headquarters of Boyd and Co. He was guided straight to the office of Mr Charles Bannana Hammock, Vice President, Strategy. The two exchanged a few pleasantries and soon shifted focus to business. For the next hour or so, the two engaged in an absorbing dialogue where Master was right on top of his game.

'Well Siddharth, you have a vision for our company and honestly I am quite impressed.'

'Thank you Charles. And let me just tell you, the kind of potential Boyd and Co has and the amount of expertise we have, we can take it to another level of value creation,' stated Master in a passionate yet rational tone.

'Siddharth, I'll be very honest with you. We are in sync on almost everything, except for one reservation that I have,' said Charles.

'I don't quite endorse the corporate social responsibility aspect of your proposal. Let's be clear Siddharth, our mission is to give to the world the best resources, the best products.'

'CSR,' he spelled out loud. 'Yes, we have a division for that which is doing its job. Serving the needy, empowering the youth and building a society—all this sugar-coated jazz looks great in seminars and summits, but that's about it, Siddharth,' said Charles.

Master had anticipated this and did not give up. He gave his best shot to explain how CSR could actually help the business grow even more holistically.

'Charles, I know where you're going. But this is different. You see, all my clients weren't too keen on having CSR as their bedrock at one time, but then they realized that CSR actually makes good business sense more than anything else,' said Master.

'That's not how I see it, Siddharth. And honestly, Boyd and Co is not one of the companies, you just talked about,' said Charles in a dismissive manner.

'All your clients put together don't stand anywhere compared to our market capitalisation, to be brutally honest,' he added.

'Charles, I don't say have CSR initiatives and be the saviour of humanity. I say go for CSR because it'll help you build a far more credible brand. Let's look at the bigger picture, Charles. In a domain like retail, what counts in the long run is the brand image you create and that's something companies aren't able to build even after spending millions on improving their services and operations. Boyd and Co, in this scenario, can have a clutter-breaking identity of trust and pro-society. Many a times conglomerates like yours complain about not having the best of talent. I say, go and create them. How can CSR not be a powerful tool? Well, finance a young kid's education, get him groomed at the best of places and sign a contract to have him on board once he's done with his education.' Master was at his persuasive best and he didn't give up right till the end.

After a discussion of over two hours, it all came down to a point where neither of them was ready to budge. Charles asked Master one final time, 'Okay, so is Siddharth-minus-the-CSR-affinity on board with us?'

'Charles, minus the CSR affinity, there is no Siddharth,' came a quick reply from Master.

That statement said everything about Master. The man had so much conviction in his beliefs that he turned down an offer which had the potential to open the floodgates for many heavy weight clients.

However, a-so-close-yet-so-far experience like this is never too good for a man's psyche, no matter how resolute he is.

It took a while for Master to get over this speed bump and what helped most was a much desired good news that came from a relatively unexpected quarter—Grinnel's. Master's alma mater had decided to incorporate his Gardener's Dilemma theory in their college syllabus. It was a matter of great honour for him and more than that, it was a huge potential opening for him to make a mark.

Gardner's Dilemma pretty soon became the talk of the town in academic circles. Articles, journals, newspapers, all had some information or the other about it. In fact it was trending all over the net.

Master left no stone unturned in cashing in on this. Under the umbrella of Gardener's Dilemma, Master quietly and craftily raised contentious issues like labour rights and the role of corporate social responsibility for all-round growth. What he was very shrewdly doing was building a public opinion on these issues and in this entire pursuit he built some valuable business relationships.

And then what caught Master's attention was the glaring labour wage problem in Goa. The labour class in Goa was reasonably discontent with their wages. Master's pen began doing the talking as many dailies and magazines woke up to this reality. This, however, didn't strike a very good chord with industrialists and certain sections of the Ministry. Master's entire endeavour actually assumed greater relevance the day he met Francescan Edwards, the labour minister of Goa.

They had a chance meeting at an economic summit organized in Mumbai where Master was a keynote speaker.

It was a typical stuffy humid day in Mumbai where the economic summit was happening in a jam-packed auditorium in the suburbs. Master was seated right next to Edwards. As the two exchanged their cards Edwards pleasantly said, 'Hey, I've read about you and your take on welfare economics.' Master gently nodded in affirmation.

Edwards continued, 'And you know what, you're the most overrated person around today.' Master was completely zapped by Edwards' casually spoken slanderous remark. 'Oh and are you some international rating agency?' asked Master mockingly.

'I am happy being Edwards. At least I don't stake tall claims,' he said and walked off.

Master couldn't quite believe his ears. Somebody for the first time had scorned him for no visible reason. Along with that, he had left Master in a strange quandary. He was curious to know why this man was so cynical about Master's consultancy and its vision. So much so, that on his return to

Goa, instead of going home he went straight to the labour ministry's office to meet Edwards.

Master entered the office and pushed in his business card at the counter. However, to Master's surprise, the man didn't meet him for two hours. Master couldn't handle this as he went berserk at the reception counter, until finally he was called in by Edwards.

Before Master could begin to speak Edwards interjected by saying, 'Listen Siddharth, our wage prices haven't been revised for a while, even though inflation is rising through the roof. Does this come under welfare economics or not?'

'It does,' replied Master.

'Well, I guess that's a serious miss,' remarked Edwards.

Master sighed for a second, looked him in the eye and asked, 'How much time has it been since you have been struggling with this?'

'Four years roughly. Can you imagine it still goes unnoticed?' grumbled Edwards.

'Doesn't raising a systematic voice, engaging in a dialogue and creating consensus amongst your government come under your purview,' asked Master in a flaring tone.

In a hesitant tone, Edwards replied, 'Well, it does. But I don't run the government.'

'Oh you did nothing except for conducting baseless self pity sessions. It has been a lame approach and that is actually what you call a serious miss,' asserted Master in a commanding tone.

He gave Edwards his piece of mind. Edwards just sat quietly in his chair and didn't say a word to counter Master's fury. Master's fiery rhetoric was followed by a stunned silence of two minutes after which Edward quietly said, 'Sunday evening, 8 p.m., same place.'

'Make that 7,' replied Master.

'Sure,' came the reply as Master got up and walked out of his office.

~

Master's nights were now getting longer and longer and slowly his study was converted into a full-blown conference room. Meetings, conferences and brainstorming continued till the wee hours of the morning.

On one such morning Sakshi and Master were sipping hot tea and catching up with each other.

'You know, Sakshi, this issue has the potential to change the way people see labour,' said Master.

'I mean, think about it, these guys deserve better pay. That's good economics in every sense,' claimed Master.

'Okay and what is good marriage, honey?' asked Sakshi in a very calm manner.

'Sitting together and having tea,' quietly answered Master.

'Let me elaborate, discussing economics over tea, isn't that a good marriage?' commented Sakshi.

'Oh. Sounds like a very cool couple to me. You know them?' remarked Master.

'Oh yes, I know them and I also know how hard it is to be one of them, Siddharth,' said Sakshi with a straight face.

Master didn't quite know how to react and empathizing with her in a guilt-ridden tone, he humbly accepted, 'You are right, it is tough.'

Sakshi quietly got up and headed straight to the bedroom. An hour later Master headed to his office for an important meeting. He sat in the driver's seat and tuned into the radio.

Harsh signal mismatch sounds while tuning the radio

channel completely turned Master off. He was about to give up when a certain thumb manoeuvre got him listening to a familiar voice.

'Ladies and gentlemen, boys and girls, children of all ages. A big hello and a very good morning from Goa's very own Jack and by the way, that's my name,' he laughed.

Master couldn't stop smiling. He hadn't heard from Jack for a very long time.

'So Goa, this is my first day here on my show *Jack's thy Answer* and honestly this show is about nothing. That's right, we will just sit here and do nothing but blabber and speak whatever we want to except for cuss words, which I honestly am fine with but our sponsors aren't.'

Master was really happy to see that Jack hadn't changed one bit. He was charming as ever and he had everyone in splits with his radio antics as well.

However, laughter and humor weren't the only things, the show was about. The first caller from Miramar colony of Goa asked Jack for advice on his relationship with his spouse.

Jack quite beautifully articulated his response and said, 'Vicky, the thing is, sometimes we take a lot of things for granted. At times we are so lost in our world that the things closest to us start blurring. It seems very minor in the beginning. You seem to ignore it but slowly that minor thing becomes a stupid awkward thing. And this awkward thing has a very twisted friend called ego. Before you know it, matters become complicated and suddenly that blurry thing is gone... it disappears forever.'

Jack spoke with so much heart that one could literally hear his heart beat across the radio.

'So guys, please don't ignore this minor thing and as far

as my minor thing is concerned, ladies and gentlemen, I just want to say one thing to my wife who's at home. Samantha, I know you are mad at me. Honestly, I don't blame you. Had I been you, I would've kicked the shit out of this idiot Jack, but the fact is, I cannot be you,' said an emotional Jack.

There was hardly a person in the recording room or the radio station who wasn't tongue-tied and hooked to the show.

'To cut the story short, wherever you are, whatever you do, today for once just go home and tell your loved one how wonderfully amazing he or she is. This is Jack and Goa, I love you very much. Keep rocking until we meet again,' signed off Jack.

The radio station broke into rapturous applause as everyone rallied around Jack and congratulated him on the start of a fresh innings. Master was so excited that he could barely keep himself planted in the driver's seat. And then suddenly something struck him and he took a sharp U-turn.

Master drove back to his place and went straight to Sakshi.

'Did you leave something at home?' asked Sakshi.

Master didn't say a word. He just went closer to her and gave her a warm hug. Nothing was asked, nothing was answered, just a simple warm hug.

Jack, on the other hand, was in a different orbit. His first day on radio was a rip-roaring success. Samantha came down to the station and post Jack's resignation from his hacking job, it was the first time the couple really got along.

'Sweetie, you were amazing,' said Samantha.

Jack held her hand and said, 'Told you, I can be quite an RJ.'

'And I'm sorry for being mad at you,' said Samantha.

'Chuck it. I am over that. Right now, I'm just living a

dream I had in my childhood when a rich baritone across the radio used to be my best friend,' smiled Jack.

'I am so happy,' gushed Samantha as she affectionately pulled his cheeks.

'Oh baby, we are going somewhere with this,' said Jack.

'You bet! Big boy,' teased Samantha.

The two had a nice dinner and it was most heartening to see them back together.

⌔

Master met Edwards for dinner as planned and the discussions on labour rights, wage policies and Goa politics in general started.

'This issue has the potential to change the political and economic landscape of the state,' said Master and one could gauge by the intensity of his words that he meant business.

'Look, it could very easily be just another flash in the pan,' said Edwards.

'Edwards, you're not seeing what I can.' One could sense a vision, a purpose taking shape in Master's mind.

'If we are taking this up, we are taking this far and it will sweep everybody into it. Corporate houses, ministries, government, labour force, everybody,' asserted Master.

'What are we waiting for then?' asked Edwards.

'An appointment with the chief of the state advisory committee,' said Master.

'That won't be an issue. Your columns have already set the temperature high, so I guess he won't be able to avoid you,' said Edwards.

'We need to roast it a bit further, Edwards. I don't want to keep this entire exercise confined to labour rights. That'll be amateurishly myopic. I want this to be about society welfare, about welfare economics in totality,' spoke Master in a commanding baritone which exuded dollops of unrelenting passion and resolve.

Edwards heard him with great attention as Master looked all pumped up to start this crusade.

Luckily Master got an appointment to meet the State Advisory Chief the next day. Master had been preparing for this crucial meeting for a while.

Guided by the peon, Master entered the Chief's cabin and to his surprise he discovered that it was none other than Vincent Nazareth.

'Oh Mr Siddharth Rane, from Grinnel's, how should I welcome you?' said Vincent Nazareth. Master battled a shattering experience and calmly said, 'It's an honour, Sir.'

'Is it?' asked Vincent. 'Or should I say "was it",' he sarcastically rephrased.

For a minute Master was absolutely dumbstruck and everything from there seemed downhill. However, he wasn't ready to let this moment go. He mustered up some courage and even though his inner self was anxious and nervous, he spoke in a firm and unwavering tone.

'It certainly was. Maybe I didn't realize it back then but honour it was nevertheless.'

'What do you want?' he asked in a very blunt tone.

Master didn't let the curtness affect him and said, 'Your help, Sir. I need it and above all Goa needs it,' smiled Master. Vincent didn't smile and did absolutely nothing to make him feel comfortable. He got up from his seat and asked Master to come along. Master didn't have a clue about where he was taking him.

After passing through half a dozen corridors, Master was guided to a conference room where ten to fifteen delegates were seated. Master greeted them. Vincent told Master, 'These people here are the advisory council to the state. For you obviously they're myopic punks, right?' asked Vincent.

Master didn't reply. Vincent however was in no sparing mood.

'Years back I visited this person's college. Though usually I am the one who is giving out some pearls of wisdom, that day someone else was being quite a jeweler,' said Vincent. The council laughed and were relishing this. Master was feeling more embarrassed with every passing minute as Vincent continued, 'He is a giant economist. Wizard, you see. He understands economics more than policy makers, finance ministers and economists.'

'Can you beat that?' he sarcastically asked.

Master by now had had enough and he decided to leave the place. Just when he was about to leave, Vincent stopped him and said, 'You know what pissed me off most that day?'

'My face,' asked Siddharth rather defensively.

'Quite close, but no,' said Vincent. He continued, 'What pissed me off most that day was the fact that everything you uttered made perfect sense and I had absolutely no answer to it.'

The entire council was shocked to hear this. Master honestly didn't know whether he was being sarcastic or he meant it.

'This son of a gun, I'm afraid to say, is gifted with one of the most uncluttered economic minds I have ever come across,' declared Vincent.

Master didn't see that coming. He heaved a huge sigh of relief and couldn't quite believe his ears. Filled with pride and honour, he chose to remain focused on his goal. After this wonderful ice-breaking, Master and Vincent discussed the labour wages issue at length. There were suggestions, contemplations and above all partnerships at various levels to tackle them.

For the next, year and a half Master worked closely with the advisory council. All eyes were on the next state budget. Master, Edwards and Vincent were leaving no stone unturned to ensure a labour rate revision in the year's state budget. Despite all the pain-staking efforts the year before, they couldn't cross the line. However, the consensus within the Advisory Council, State Ministry and the common citizens of Goa had increased manifold the following year.

Master had invested his last drop of blood, sweat and tears into this. So high were the stakes that Master had turned into an insomniac. He'd roam all night like a zombie. The countdown for the state budget announcement had begun.

'I was nervous. I was excited. I didn't know where we were heading. Amidst all this I got the good news that I was to become a father soon. A lot was happening indeed. Sakshi kept telling me that I shall overcome this but the truth was that for this one final thing we had given all that we had. And perhaps this was it! I was way too overwhelmed by the moment and one day while on one of my stress-busting long morning walks I realized that Jack's radio station was just about a kilometer away from

there. Ah! I don't know what happened, how it happened, I just walked on and reached the radio station to meet Jack, whom I hadn't seen in years.'

⌢

Master requested the radio staff to allow him in and after much persuasion he was guided inside. As he entered the inner lobby, he looked across the glass of the recording room and saw Jack standing there.

Jack also saw him and for a second completely fumbled on the mike. He couldn't stop smiling. He took off the recording apparatus and rushed out.

The staff around was absolutely baffled to see Jack outside the recording room when the show was on air.

'Man...oh, man,' shouted Jack as he ran towards Master and hugged him tightly.

The two had so much to say, so much to talk about but amidst all this, a sizeable chunk of Goa's population tuned into 92.8 was feeling left out. So Jack got back in and also tagged Master along with him inside the recording room.

'So Goa, Jack is back and today I have a friend with me joining us. He has been my inspiration. And yet I haven't met him in years, despite staying in the same city,' Jack said, exhaling a puff of air. 'I know I'm such a loser! But you don't be like me because if you have a friend in town, bring him home and chit-chat till one of you dozes off,' advised Jack on a lighter note.

He warmly continued, 'Nevertheless, allow me to introduce to you a great economist, a socially conscious individual, my friend Siddharth Rane, or as some of you may know him, Master.'

Master wasn't expecting this to happen but then, when

you're with Jack you don't expect, you just flow. In his characteristic deep baritone, Master greeted Goa and thanked Jack, who went on to narrate some funny college incidents and memories which the two shared.

After a nostalgia trip and a few laughs, Jack put aside everything and talked business.

'You see friends, Siddharth for me would've stayed Siddharth had he just been a phenomenal economist who works for a top notch corporate house and makes a killing for himself and his family. But the man sitting next to me isn't Siddharth. For the world he ceased to be Siddharth the day he announced he will be society's gardener instead of being an economist. That's when Master was born for the world. For me, well it was slightly earlier,' he said with a wink towards Master.

Master was absolutely honoured by Jack's kind words. He acknowledged Jack and then spoke at length about the core issue of labour wages in particular and other societal issues in general.

He ended on the note, 'I know, to some of you all this jazz regarding economics, society, labour and wages sounds much like another load of intellectual crap, but trust me, it affects us.'

Jack grabbed the microphone and said, 'Sure as hell, it affects us and that's why we are supporting them.'

Clearing his throat, he said, 'Enough surprises for the day. Just one last thing, this is Jack signing off from *Jack's thy Answer* and though I say it every day I never really get tired of saying that Goa, I love you.'

.8.

Nirvana at 30

Inside the green room of the recording studio Jack sat on the couch with his head thrown back staring at the ceiling above. Some of his colleagues sitting around him were throwing around ideas about how they could make the slots more interesting. The room was abuzz with suggestions, cross analysis and ideas. However, Jack was absolutely oblivious to what was happening, which was very unlike him. For a long time, he didn't say a word and went straight to the program director Ryan.

'Ryan, what's up with that social show *Goa Matters*. You were planning to bring it up in the morning slot right?'

'It's a great show, Jack and I really think it'll be a great interface between the people and state officials,' claimed Ryan.

'Is it ready?' asked Jack.

'Ready and sealed, but we don't have a slot. The kind of numbers you're bringing in are incredible. We won't mess with that,' he smiled.

'Ah right,' said Jack with a sporting smile.

For some reason, that whole day Jack felt out of sorts. This continued for a couple of days and on one such evening, he and Samantha went out for a breather to Imperial Night Club.

The ambience at Imperial was always fresh and thematic. The theme that night was rebel, an instinct Jack connected with quite religiously.

The two sat down for a couple of margaritas and a feast of prawns. For a major part of the day, Jack had been silent and this hadn't gone unnoticed with Samantha.

She asked him, 'Everything okay, Jack?'

'Yeah, sort of. In fact yes, everything is okay,' replied Jack who still appeared lost and bewildered.

'What is it, Jack?' said Samantha placing her hand on Jack's palm.

'Samantha, I have an amazing radio show.'

'True,' she replied.

'An amazingly fantastic wife,' exclaimed Jack.

'Absolutely,' she replied with a warm smile.

'And everything is good but, then something is missing. I don't know what it is,' sighed Jack.

Samantha affectionately rubbed his hand and said, 'Honey, you always complicate things. The world around is simpler, much simpler than you think. We can keep it simple and live like normal people, happy and satisfied with what we have.'

'Samantha, had I kept it normal, I would've never had you. I would've never had anything, if I had kept it normal. Whether it was the fun of hacking into networks or talking live on the radio, nothing would've happened,' said Jack with a beaming smile.

'There's no point arguing with you. I was stupid to try,' said Samantha.

Jack smiled and before he could say anything, there was the electric sound of a strumming guitar. Following the guitar, were throbbing drumbeats and out came some rebel-stamped music. The band's name was 'Nirvana at 30' and there was rebel written all over their music, their dressing and mannerisms.

Besides some of their own not-so-popular compositions, they performed classics like "Highway to Hell" by ACDC and of course the legendary "They don't care about us" by Michael Jackson.

The MJ-holic Jack couldn't stop himself from grooving. As Jack got up, he felt a sudden burst of adrenaline in his veins, something he hadn't felt in years. The kind, he had perhaps experienced last at Grinnel's.

For that moment, that instant, Jack honestly wasn't aware of what he was doing, not that he was aware otherwise, but it was in such detached-with-reality situations that Jack was at his best. He walked up to the band, hugged their lead singer and other band members and mingled with them in no time.

Samantha just looked on in surprise, trying to understand what Jack was up to. Something she had been doing ever since Jack had entered her life. Jack, meanwhile, grabbed a microphone and started, 'Good evening, Goa. This is Jack.'

The words instantly rang a bell with the audience. The only difference being that they were used to hearing them early morning instead of in the evening.

The response from the audience made Jack feel a lot more relaxed and at home as he casually held the microphone, walked around and spoke straight from his heart.

'Guys, you see such is the amazing rush of being a rebel that if rebellion isn't the scene in heaven, I want to gate-crash hell,' said Jack in a hoarse power-packed voice.

'Nirvana at 30, you are awesome. Watching you guys reminded me of my college days when some of my friends and I used to jam and come up with random music. I had written one song, I remember, which must be lying in some rusty corner of my room or it might just be lost, I don't know.

But what I do know for sure is that it's here,' said Jack, pointing to his heart.

'Today I want to relive that moment and sing that song,' said Jack. The crowd cheered for him and so did the band members. Samantha smiled and joined the brigade cheering for him.

Jack cleared his throat and cautiously spoke, 'Pardon me, in case I bullshit, cause I am not really that good. I just want you guys to help me sail through this one.'

The cheers grew louder as Jack clapped his hands together and out came the song "Banjara Main". Perhaps the song still echoed in the backyards of Grinnel's.

'Banjara main, banjara yeh sama.' Jack's voice didn't support his gusto on a couple of notes, but so charged was the moment that these technicalities mattered little. The crowd joined in and Jack sang along with the audience. He was all over the place. Interspersed between the lyrics were his constant witty jibes which added spice to the performance.

Moving through the entire length and breadth of the audience, he came to his wife. 'Ladies and gentlemen, the buck of my life indeed stops here,' he funnily stated.

'Yes, this is my wife. And every day she wishes, I was not a rebel,' he laughed.

'But thank God I am a rebel because otherwise she would have never been Jack's Samantha,' smiled Jack. Samantha couldn't stop blushing and all she could say was, 'You are beyond madness.' The crowd completely enjoyed the moment and gave them a standing ovation.

Next morning, just like any other day, Jack walked into the

radio station, ready and geared up for his show. As things were being put in place, he sat back-stage sipping his morning coffee. He seemed much calmer and more content that day.

Sharp at 7, Jack in his characteristic style greeted Goa with his trademark, 'Good morning, Goa. This is Jack and you are with me here on *Jack's thy Answer*.' Those words, every morning gave people more of a kick than perhaps their morning tea and this day was no different. Just like any other day, Jack attended a few calls, cracked a few jokes and effortlessly entertained people.

As Jack started approaching the end of yet another episode of the show he said, 'Guys for the last year, year and a half, I've been an outlet of sorts to your emotions, your feelings. You just came and said anything you wanted to say, share or talk about. And it has been fun. There have been days when we've laughed and then there have been days when we've laughed even harder,' smiled Jack.

'We shall always laugh, no matter what. That's the only thing I did when I dropped out of Grinnel's. I had nothing in my hand, nowhere to go, not a penny and guess what I did. I got married,' Jack laughed.

Everybody was in splits. They carefully heard him and could sense that the conversation was heading somewhere.

'The world is a crazy place and the only way you can beat it is by being crazier. But with greater craziness comes greater responsibility. Yes, that's what the new age crazy Spiderman would say,' he chuckled.

'No, seriously. If you are laughing and smiling, make sure people around you are also doing the same. That's what the spirit of Goa stands for. We laugh, we party and we make sure no one is left behind. Yes, there are problems and issues that are perhaps serious. At times serious enough to take our smile away. But we will not let that happen. We'll address these issues, stand united and fight for our smile, come what may,' said Jack with a beaming smile that spread across many homes and many people that morning.

'So, just keep smiling and keep fighting against these smile-stealing problems. And…one more thing guys…Today is my last day,' stated Jack with a smile that didn't really spread across the people around him this time.

'What the hell was that?' was the remark repeated by all the unit members and listeners.

'It has been a fun ride, guys. But hey, that in no way means we are done, because some other place, some other time, we'll meet again. Till then keep smiling and keep rocking. This is Jack and Goa, I love you very much,' he signed off with one final hurrah.

The backstage staff was waiting for the show to end and then they barged into the recording room. They all bombarded Jack with questions. None of them listened, until Jack finally stood up on his recording chair and said, 'Guys…guys…we've made one hell of a show. First let's cheer for that. I know you're mad at me but the fact is that it is time for this ship to sail on…'

Ryan interrupted, 'Jack didn't want me to tell you guys about this but he gave me his resignation a week back.'

Jack said, 'Come on guys, I wanted to go out with a bang and guess what, there's a new ship ready to join you on the coastline. This young lad has come up with a phenomenal social show, *Goa Matters*. Let's give it up for him.'

'His show will be an extension of *Jack's thy Answer*. It's a lot more meaningful than what I've been doing,' Jack continued.

One of the other RJs asked Jack, 'What are you going to do from tomorrow, Jack?'

Jack replied with a smile, 'I think I have an idea but let us not go there. Let's talk about today.' Jack's volume went up a little as he slipped into a celebratory mood and called out to everyone.

Ryan had already planned a farewell party for Jack at the Imperial. Amidst all the fun Jack climbed onto the stage and like always he poured his heart out.

'Thank you everyone, especially Ryan for sticking with me despite my repeated goof ups with the sound button. Somehow I pulled it off and guess what, from next week there will be something else I'll be trying to pull off.'

'In fact,' wondered Jack. 'Why wait till next week, let me give it a shot today,' declared Jack, smiling on his way to the back arena.

Jack's friends and colleagues were all curious to know what he was going to do and every one waited in anticipation. A few moments later, Jack walked back with an electric guitar and oodles of attitude, surprising everyone with his new avatar. Jack was a bundle of nerves, as evident from his jittery body language, but he still went ahead.

He gently seated himself and having set the mike accordingly he nervously strummed the strings with a degree of uncertainty. Though the reception was warm Jack could sense that something just wasn't right. He, however, continued and tried to sing "Summer of 69". However, what came out was everything but music. Oblivious to this Jack enthusiastically asked people to sing along with him. Most of them couldn't quite figure out the song. As far as the others were concerned, there were hardly any two people singing the same song.

Unfortunately for Jack it wasn't his day. Alas! So embarrassing was the sight that even a sport like Jack couldn't do much.

However, one man and one team who couldn't afford an embarrassment then was Master and his group. It was the night before the state budget was to be announced.

'I still remember that day quite vividly. None of us, neither me nor Edwards, nor Vincent, had slept the night before. All eyes were on the state budget that was to be presented in the state assembly that day.'

Vincent and his advisory team were convinced that the labour price hike would indeed happen. Master had gone completely silent. Thoughts ranging from "I couldn't have done anymore" to "what if my best is actually not enough" flashed through his mind. Added to this was the fact that Sakshi was in her ninth month of pregnancy and expecting to deliver any time.

'We'll make it, Siddharth. Don't worry. Everybody was game for our proposal and it is going to happen,' said Vincent very calmly.

Master didn't reply. He didn't even nod or make eye contact with anyone. He just got up and went out to get some fresh air. He was pensively strolling in the verandah when he received a phone call from his mother. He picked up the phone and said, 'The budget is not out yet.'

His mother replied in a rather excited tone, 'Siddharth, come home soon.'

'Is Sakshi alright?' enquired Master.

'She's in labour. You are about to become a father,' exclaimed Mrs Rane with both excitement and a tinge of worry.

'Ah...okay, I am coming to the hospital. You take care,' said Master, huffing and puffing in excitement.

Vincent shouted from inside, 'Siddharth...'

Master didn't reply. Instead he grabbed his keys and headed straight to his car.

Vincent and Edwards were left wondering what happened, as they quickly went in and attended calls to gather news of the budget which had by now started trickling in.

Master's phone, meanwhile, was busy beeping with call alerts and messages. He wasn't going to attend to anyone except Sakshi then.

Meanwhile, pandemonium broke loose at Master's office as the state budget continued to unravel. And then came the big news. There were no subsidies for the poor. Despite rising inflation there was no revision in the labour wages. On the contrary, there was a significant hike in the prices of many vital commodities.

Edwards and Vincent didn't say a word, nor did they exchange any glances. Edwards was disappointed to see their efforts go completely down the drain. He had assured the various labour unions of a wage revision. He was so embarrassed that he couldn't muster up the courage to meet them or attend their calls.

Vincent wasn't expecting a complete deaf ear to all the recommendations of his advisory council. He called for an urgent meeting to discuss what could be done next. Master, however, was completely oblivious to everything. He wasn't attending any calls or messages and was busy playing the family man.

As he rushed inside Goa Medical Hospital, he saw his parents waiting outside the ward. They were all excited yet nervous and so was Master, for whom it had been an emotionally draining day thus far.

They waited anxiously for the good news. It was surprising to see a workaholic economist like Master not care for what supposedly was his most important day at work.

Every second seemed like a light year to Master. His phone meanwhile had crashed due to the nonstop phone calls and messages. But after all the crashing and anxiety came the news they had all been waiting for. The Rane family was blessed with a Master Junior.

Sakshi was still recuperating as Master sat next to her and the two shared a warm moment. 'Thank you so much, Sakshi,' stated Master gently kissing her as he held her hand. Sakshi seemed drained of energy but her smile didn't waver. Master held his little one in his hands and looked at him wondering with surprise, 'I can't believe he fits in my palm.'

Master's mother laughed and said, 'Son, you too used to fit in right there.'

Master was amazed and tried to absorb all the joy of becoming a father.

After a while Sakshi asked, 'Siddharth, what about the budget? What happened?'

'Oh...I have no clue,' said Master exhaling to ease his anxiety.

'My phone crashed and I'm completely disconnected. But it's okay. I am connected with everyone who matters to me today in my life,' smiled Master.

Mr and Mrs Rane were happy to hear their workaholic son's priorities. However, much to everyone's surprise Sakshi said,

'Honey, you have to be connected. What's wrong with you?'

'Excuse me, is this coming from you?' smiled Master.

'Yeah, it's coming from me. Call up Vincent, Edwards or whoever and find out,' asserted Sakshi.

'Yeah, I will do that but honestly, right now nothing matters to me,' said Master.

Master borrowed his father's phone and called Vincent and then Edwards. None of them took his call so he called the research analyst of his firm and enquired about the state budget.

That is when he found out that Vincent had resigned from the advisory council. Edwards too had relinquished his post of labour minister. Master's plans and initiatives had been thrown into the bin by the state government. There were reports of backlash amongst the labour class whose high hopes were completely dashed.

Master's worst fear had just come true. Over the phone he didn't react but went silent for a few minutes after he hung up. Sakshi could make out that something had gone terribly wrong.

'Siddharth, what happened?' asked Sakshi.

Master didn't react for a while and then said, 'Nothing. Nothing happened. We are done and it's all over.'

Sakshi was slightly puzzled at Master's strange behaviour.

'What do you mean?' asked a slightly worried and confused Sakshi.

'None of our proposals were accepted. Edwards has quit and so has Vincent. There are labour backlashes,' explained Master.

'We were being fooled all this while. What were we thinking when we thought of fighting the system?' wondered Master in a resigned tone.

He continued, 'But honey, don't worry. I'll set it all straight. Nothing is damaged. I'll wrap up this fight-the-system shit and take up something more productive for us. I'm not putting our family's future in jeopardy for my foolish convictions.'

Sakshi couldn't quite believe her ears and was absolutely dumbstruck at Master's complete metamorphosis. She was also worried at Master's strange behaviour. She held herself and knew it was time for her to step in.

'Siddharth, how long have we known each other?' asked Sakshi, looking him in the eye.

'Twenty years,' replied Master.

'Yes, twenty years is a long time. Over the years we've been through a lot, Siddharth. Some good days, some not so good. There have been days when you didn't even come home. Remember our third anniversary when I kept waiting and you didn't make it.'

'Honey, I apologized for that,' replied Master.

'No, that's not the point. Listen to me...' she said in an uncharacteristically aggressive tone.

'What happened? Is everything okay?' asked a slightly perturbed Master.

'No. What happened to you, Siddharth? For the past twenty years I did not mind missing out on an anniversary celebration or a nice dinner with you or spending Christmas with you because every single day we were both living your dream. Damn it! We were living your conviction which today you just want to throw out of the window for your family.'

Master tried to calm her down. 'But Sakshi...'

'No. You listen to me today. For the last twenty years, I didn't complain even once because I thought your conviction is worth it. Today you are no one, absolutely no one to toss it out of the window just because of one failure or one new entrant to our family,' shouted Sakshi.

Master was completely silenced by Sakshi's fiery rhetoric. The silence soon gave way to deep introspection.

'Honey, but I did give it my all, didn't I?' asked Master.

'I can't believe this is the same man who thought losing is not an option. Siddharth, you didn't give up in the Math Olympiad when you were stacked against students bigger and more qualified than you, did you? Dammit, you are the one who looked Vincent in the eye and told him "It's not working, Sir". You are the man who made Gardener's Dilemma reach text books even when the most learned ones had dismissed it as some weird figment of your imagination and today you just want to chicken out because two men resigned and some protested,' asserted Sakshi.

Never before, had Master seen Sakshi in this avatar as he just kept quiet and absorbed all of it.

That day, in that hospital ward, my entire life flashed before my eyes. It was one of those moments, when I actually thought of throwing in the towel and had it not been for Sakshi that day I wouldn't be sitting here before you. A lot of people say "You're a tough person". Well, all I can tell them is you haven't met my wife'.

The people laughed and this momentary laughter was a pleasant change in Master's intense narrative. The narrative went on as Master continued spilling the beans on what happened next.

132 • *Jack & Master*

There was pin-drop silence in the ward. Sakshi had spoken her heart out and Master didn't say a word. He was as vulnerable as a man could get. Standing at a crossroads in life with a wife and a child to take care of, with a professional vision that had never been more blurred, Master just sat down and closed his eyes for a while. Every single word that Sakshi had said continued ringing bells in his mind. He knew how much his conviction meant to him. However, a knee-jerk failure and the realization of fatherhood had blinded his reason and conviction. Master kept reasoning with himself and slowly and steadily the remnants of passion which were buried deep inside him came to life. Inch by inch, they joined each other and slowly started taking shape. Master was still perplexed. He got up from his seat and went out for a walk. Every single step he took had more resolve than the previous one. The shape by now had started assuming greater proportions. The fact and belief that he always strived for nothing less than excellence in his work dawned on him. The fact that ever since he had gained understanding of economics, welfare economics had been his sole passion and belief kept popping up. The proportions by now were monumentous and volcanic. Master recalled everything he had ever achieved, all he had been through, all his dreams and beliefs and then in one defiant tone, he said to himself, 'It isn't over. Dammit! It isn't over.' Master was ready to take on the world.

∫

'I still get goose bumps when I look back at that day. I realized back then that my wife and family responsibility would never hold me back. In fact, never had I needed their support and strength more.'

Master went back to the ward after his walk. Sakshi had been worried by his absence and was glad to see him back. However, she wasn't able to guess his state of mind.

Master immediately called for someone to get his phone in order. One could see a considerable change in his body language.

Master was in no mood to sit back. Looking at his little one, he quietly smiled, went to Sakshi, held her hand and gave her an assuring smile and a nod. Sakshi just smiled back and reciprocated the nod. Her eyes were resolute enough to tell Master, 'Go and fight the world, I'm with you.'

Men like Master do not crumble very easily and if ever they go down, they go down very deep. Deep enough to either drown or to emerge as an insurmountable force. This force steered its way to the labour ministry office. The atmosphere there was very hostile. There were labour representatives crowding outside the office and Master knew it wasn't a very good time to be there. However, he was ready to take it all on his chin. He frantically kept looking for Edwards, whose resignation had spurred even more chaos.

The union leader, A.N. Mistry, stopped Master on his way and confronted him, 'What do I tell the people now? What do I tell the hundreds and thousands of skilled and unskilled labourers in Goa who were assured some sort of respite by you guys?'

He continued in a loud tone, 'Should I tell them it's all over?'

Master tried to calm him down but to no avail as he continued insulting Master, rather irrationally.

'You bloody intellectuals are placed on a far higher pedestal by us than you really deserve,' argued Mistry.

Fuelled by his consistent verbal slander Master flew off the handle and said, 'Listen Mr Mistry or whatever they call you, I am not here to present you or anyone here with my intellectual credentials. Because quite frankly, you won't get it and neither will your cynical side-kicks who do nothing but whine and bad-mouth anyone who is making an effort.'

'Are you done putting the onus here?' argued Mistry.

'My priority isn't to point fingers but to unite them to form a fist that can weather this storm,' asserted Master.

Master's commanding baritone in the corridor of the ministry office drew attention and response from all quarters. Muffled voices from all corners started gaining momentum before Master in his characteristic dominant style declared, 'Let's not blow this up. I know it's a tough situation for you all but it isn't easy for Edwards or me either. God is my witness when I say, this is the only thing we have been working on for the last two years.'

The people stood there attentively listening to Master.

'I know we have been screwed but I promise you we will screw them back,' shouted Master in an aggressive tone.

'I won't take this lying down and neither do I want you. But hey, you have to trust me and I promise you, I will not let you down,' said Master enunciating every word distinctly and loudly. So enthused were the people in that room that the energy there was palpable.

Master stormed out and went looking for Edwards.

.9.

It Affects Us

'Not gonna stay down now,
Won't take it lying down now (strings of guitar)
Cause it's time to fly (chorus).
And I am not gonna lie cause I never felt this free before.'

The claps followed and for the first time in three weeks, Jack lived up to his own stage expectations. Unstrapping the guitar and taking a bow in front of the audience, Jack cheerfully headed towards the backstage area. He looked at his phone and saw a message from Samantha which read:

Jack, I have been thinking hard and I guess, things aren't working between us. I never thought it would come to this, but I guess I need a break. I am going to my parents' place for a while.

Jack's post-performance euphoria and excitement completely faded in seconds. But instead of sulking he immediately called up Samantha who didn't take any of his calls. For a few minutes, extending to an hour and a half Jack didn't quite realize the gravity of the situation. However, suddenly the realization of staying without Samantha hit him like a thunderbolt. A few minutes later the realization turned into panic and then it turned into a freak show. Jack immediately packed his bag and rushed to Samantha's parents' place in Mumbai.

Samantha's parents and Jack had hardly ever met since the famous eloping episode. However, that didn't deter Jack from going to their house. When Jack reached Mr and Mrs DeVilliers' place, he wasn't too sure about how he was going to greet them.

Jack rang the door-bell and waited anxiously. Mr DeVilliers opened the door and gave Jack a very disdainful look. Jack tried smiling at him which had no effect. He then said a polite 'Hi' but before he could finish, Mr DeVilliers turned his back on him and started walking inside. Jack knew he was there for a long night.

He entered and to feel accepted started a casual conversations which didn't cut ice with a rather reserved Mr DeVilliers.

'What a fantastic house you have. I have never really seen it before,' said Jack.

'Thanks for reminding us that we have a son-in-law who hasn't visited us in the last five years,' remarked Mr DeVilliers.

It wasn't the best of starts for Jack, but he continued nevertheless. 'Hey, mom-in-law, you seem to have lost a lot of weight. Is it dieting or health consciousness?'

'No, just plain and simple worry. Worry for my married daughter,' replied Mrs DeVilliers, with a deadpan look.

Every time Jack opened his mouth, he'd land up with an even bigger foot in it. Meanwhile Jack saw Samantha near the staircase and winked at her in a playful manner. Samantha turned her head the other way and started looking outside the window.

The tension and cold undercurrents were palpable and before they reached their apex, Jack clapped his hands and said, 'Alright guys, let's just talk it out.'

'Jack, there's nothing left to talk about,' said Mrs DeVilliers.

'So that means it's all sorted, right? Fair enough then, let's all go out and have a family dinner,' replied Jack.

Mr DeVilliers wasn't too impressed. He lost his patience and shouted, 'Enough screwing around, Jack. What do you think of yourself? Five years back you took away our daughter. We didn't say much because she was happy. But today, she's fed up of you and so are we.'

'Okay and what's the reason for that?' enquired Jack patiently.

'The reason is your stupidity. What the hell do you do? Strum a guitar, blabber a few words on the radio, hack a website? Who knows, tomorrow you might become a pole dancer.'

'That's actually not a bad idea at all,' laughed Jack only to receive a cold look from a not-so-impressed Mr DeVilliers. He looked towards Samantha and smiled again, but to no avail.

He then came forward on his chair, affectionately looked towards Mr DeVilliers and said, 'You know what Sir, I lost both my parents when I was fourteen.'

For a moment, there was pin-drop silence in the room. Jack sighed a little, then smiled and said, 'Since then, it has been me, pretty much on my own. My mom and dad were very meticulous parents. They used to plan everything in advance. Study time this, vacation time that, everything planned. But then life had something else planned. One accident and all their plans went for a toss.'

Jack paused for a while, leaned back on the couch, caught his breath and continued, 'That's why all I have learnt in life is to just go with the flow and in that flow make people happy and live the moment. That's all I know. I never planned to marry your daughter, it just happened and thank God it did. I never planned to be an RJ or a guitar strummer as you said. It just happened.'

Jack spoke with so much sincerity that neither Samantha nor Mrs DeVilliers moved from their places. Mr DeVilliers for the first time was actually hearing Jack out quite patiently.

'Yes, there are a few things I had planned in life. I had always thought, I'd love my wife and her parents more than anything in the world. I thought I'll make for a killer husband and a kick-ass son-in-law and they'd be lucky to have me. But alas, it kills me to see that I failed.'

Samantha was so moved by Jack's words that she couldn't hold her tears back. Jack also had a lump in his throat but he smiled and said, 'That's why I never plan. Good things always happen.'

Mr DeVilliers didn't say a word. Nevertheless he was moved, and so was Mrs DeVilliers, who avoided making eye contact with Jack.

Jack got up and said, 'I didn't come here planning to take Sam back with me. I don't want to plan this.' Jack looked towards Sam and said, 'I just hope, it happens at the right time for us.'

Samantha didn't say a word. Her moist eyes did the talking. Jack picked up his bag, winked at Sam and got moving with a hope in his heart.

If there was hope here, there was a state of complete hopelessness and restlessness in some other corner of Goa.

∽

A completely scattered study was witness to some even more scattered individuals trying to find direction.

'The local media has been quite heavy on the labour clashes in Panjim,' stated Edwards.

'The Finance Minister and his set of butt-kissers are hailing it as a pro-labour budget. In fact, sections of the media are blaming us for over-promising,' said Vincent.

Edwards agreed with Vincent and said, 'It's only a matter of time before everything dries up and things go back to normal. Labour will continue to be exploited, the lack of inclusiveness will continue and there is nothing we can do about it.'

'True, but not completely,' said Master, looking pensive.

'And what's the complete truth?' asked Vincent.

Master got up from his seat and started walking around. Deep in his thoughts he didn't say a word for a couple of minutes.

Breaking his silence he said, 'Vincent, you are right when you say everything will be forgotten soon, but as far as we doing nothing about it is concerned, we can shake the very foundation of this establishment.'

'What's up your sleeve, Siddharth? Tell me,' asked Edwards.

'Edwards, the media is being very heavy on these clashes and we know it's not going to be long before they are forgotten. Let's blow this thing through the roof and make it a Frankenstein monster,' said Master.

Master pulled back a chair, sat on it and said, 'Listen guys, we have tried things the conventional way. We had dialogues, advisory committees and God knows what. Today this issue is hot, if not red hot. Let's bring this movement to the streets. Let's make it hotter and then strike hard because that's how they'll understand.'

Master's aggression was palpable. Vincent and Edwards were trying to understand Master's perspective.

'For this we have to act very fast,' said Master. Galvanizing into action he said, 'Edwards you take back your resignation. I'm telling you, we need to have a voice in the ministry to take it forward.'

Before Edwards could say anything, Master said again, 'Vincent, it's important you address the media, explaining why you resigned and how the state government completely disregarded the proposals of the advisory committee.'

'As far as the clashes are concerned, I'll personally have a word with Mistry and try to ensure that instead of clashes, we have concerted demonstrations,' said Master.

'Siddharth…' called Vincent.

'For one last time, are you sure we're doing this? We go forward here and there'll be no turning back. We might be perceived as anarchists, sore losers and at worst we could become a spectacle of public mockery,' cautioned Vincent.

'Oh, I've never been more sure about anything in my life. We didn't come this far to throw this out of the window. If there's anything I can do for my conviction I will do it. This movement is going to the streets and it's time we turned the heat up,' said Master in his characteristic confident and definitive style.

So there in that dingy study room at the corner of Pedal Street, we decided to take this movement to the streets of Goa. It truly was a turning point of my life. From the comfortable confines of our air-conditioned offices to the dust and heat of the streets, our initiatives had come a long way,' recalled Master.

'The next few weeks saw something unprecedented and this movement united under the common creed "it affects us".'

'It affects us,' shouted James, the lead singer of Nirvana at 30.

'This song is written by Goa's very own, Jack,' declared James.

The crowd erupted with applause and the stage was set for an electrifying performance. Besides writing this song, Jack was the support guitarist in the band and would also sing a couple of lines.

The theme of the song was in sync with Goa's mood at the time. Jack's love for Goa and his understanding of its cultural values had helped him compose this song.

'Twenty miles from here, a movement is about to start. It talks about labour rights, inclusive economics and a whole lot of stuff that I know might not intrigue you,' said Jack.

'But the fact is, whether labour or not, a deprivation of rights is something we must not tolerate. Today it's about labour wages, tomorrow it could be something else. The bottom line is "It affects us",' declared Jack.

'It affects us,' the crowd shouted.

'Tomorrow, when Master and his team hit the streets, we must join them and show all the Big Daddys out there that "It affects us",' smiled Jack with enthusiasm which was contagious enough to energize the gathering.

Like any other evening in Goa, it was lively yet calm. Master's office was abuzz with activity as usual.

'The media is expected any minute, Siddharth,' said Vincent, who had for the last two weeks, been very actively addressing the media on this issue.

'Listen, get one thing very clear. Tell them we are taking this to the streets only because these people didn't settle it inside four walls. Assure them that this demonstration is going to be a peaceful one,' said Master.

'Look, I have already said it a dozen times,' said Vincent.

'Keep reiterating this, Vincent. We need to drill this in the minds of common Goans who might not be very avid news followers,' claimed Master.

'And one more thing, Vincent. You are the voice of this movement. And this voice should be of a man who is convinced that he is right and that those people sitting in the State Legislatives are wrong. You have to come across as someone who feels empowered because he is actually right and justified,' asserted Master, whose passion at that point could bring the roof down.

'Edwards won't be joining us from day one. Let the movement gather some momentum. He can then come in and give us credibility,' strategized Master.

'Will you also be addressing the media, Siddharth?' asked Vincent.

'Yes, but to a very limited extent.' He then explained, 'Vincent, this movement is uncharted territory. We have no clue about what could come our way. We cannot show all our cards together. I will, as of now just be the voice of reason in this movement.'

Master was bubbling with ideas and strategies.

'Yes, but you keep the labour unions and their heads moving,' said Vincent.

'Sure, I will get them. I am keeping in touch with Mistry and the other union heads. Don't worry' reaffirmed Master.

Before Master could even finish, his company's research

assistant, Rishi, barged into the room with some maps and paper cuttings. Rishi quickly set out the map on the table as Master and he zeroed down on the locations where the movement would garner maximum mileage.

'It was all moving very fast. And that's the beauty of movements. Either things just keep happening at break-neck speed with each brick falling in the right place or you just keep waiting and it never really takes off,' said Master.

For the crowd at India Gate, it was a learning experience to know how such a big movement was conceived, planned and eventually executed. All they remembered about the Movement was what they had seen on television and read in print.

City Centre, Goa.

It was 7 a.m. in the morning. Master, Vincent and their entire team had acquired permission to hold a peaceful demonstration and had started setting up for what was going to be a long, challenging day.

The make-shift stage was set up along with the public address system. Within no time, the media people began trickling in. In front of the stage lay mattresses and carpets where the gathering assembled. On either side of the gathering there were media persons along with their camera crew.

One of them asked Vincent what their demands were. Vincent promptly replied, 'Our immediate demand is a revision of labour wages. The minimum wages in Goa need to go up and be in sync with rising inflation.' With these words Vincent climbed the steps and reached the stage.

'So is this movement focused mainly on labour wage revision?' asked another journalist.

Master was standing a few feet away from Vincent and was quietly observing him. Suddenly something struck him and before Vincent could answer the question, he promptly intervened and asked Vincent to come along. In a very polite manner Master told the media persons that they will get back to them and address all their queries as the day progresses.

Vincent was slightly livid at Master, 'What the hell was that, Siddharth? I was in the middle of something.'

'I know. Listen you've got to understand, we cannot give away everything so early on in the day and be left with nothing new to say by the evening,' reasoned Master.

'Screw you and your logic,' said Vincent, rather disgustedly, as he walked away. However, deep down it was a point he understood well. As hours passed, labour union heads from across the state and other sections of the labour class gathered to build a decent crowd. Various social activists, philanthropists and NGOs also gave this demonstration a much needed impetus.

Master's team was pretty happy with the turn out. However, Master still wasn't satisfied. On being asked why he was worried he told his team, 'This movement is not going anywhere till the common man of Goa doesn't show up in our support. It will be just another elitist gathering where jargons like "reforms and socio-economic development" are thrown around with no connect or logical conclusion whatsoever.'

'Look Siddharth, let's not allow these things to deviate us from our plan of action right now,' said Vincent. He called Rishi to make a note of the State policies and legislations, they were to talk about.

Master was thinking really fast. In the middle of their conversation, he suddenly said, 'Listen, we have to change a few things here.'

'Siddharth, you are confusing everybody. There are people waiting out there for us. Stick to the plan,' said Vincent.

'I know I'm confused. I know that,' said Master freaking out for a second.

However, the very next second he immediately regrouped and calmly assuring everyone said, 'Listen guys, we put one step wrong and before you know it everything will fall like a pack of cards. The moment will slip away and there'll be absolutely nothing we'll be able to do about it. So try and understand that, we are not going out there tom-toming about policies, legislatures, IPCs and all these technical terms. They will not cut ice with the common man of Goa,' warned Master.

He continued, 'Our language has to be very simple and relatable to the common man.'

'Our talks will be rational no doubt, but an emotional tinge is necessary if we don't want this to die,' asserted Master with a sense of urgency.

The crowd gathered at the City Centre was eagerly waiting to be addressed by Master and Vincent as it kept getting more restless and noisy.

'I guess, that's it. We will have to go and face them,' said Vincent.

'Vincent, I will give the keynote speech. You take it from there and remember, keep it crisp and relatable,' reiterated Master as he marched towards the stage.

He was welcomed by a round of applause as he grabbed a microphone and kick started the movement that was going to change his fate forever.

'I have always believed in growth and development. Nothing should stop it. But what is this growth? What is this development? We keep talking about it. Is it the six, seven or eight point something number called GDP? Or is it the fact that every single citizen is getting what he or she deserves?' asked Master in an emphatic manner. 'If it is the latter you are all at the right place.'

The claps continued and so did Master. 'A lot of people are asking us, what is your demand? What is this "It affects us" movement all about?'

'Well, to set it all straight, I'll say loud and clear that this movement is about Goa, the state of our dreams. We all love this state and wish for two things. One, that everybody gets what he or she deserves and two, that everybody becomes deserving enough. The first can happen only if our rights are protected and the second can happen only if the established individuals and corporate houses take it upon themselves to help the needy. Today we are here to take up the first— protection of our rights; the rights of our labourers who have been denied their due time and again despite rising inflation and despite the recommendations of the advisory council.'

Master had beautifully and articulately set up the entire backdrop of the movement in his speech.

'We can either go down the "let's accept it" way or we can tell them in one voice that we will not be cowed down this time because "It affects us", declared Master in a thunderous voice which echoed across the television channels and the news papers the next day.

The movement started on a decent note, however, sustaining the momentum was the real challenge.

.10.

It Affects Us–II

'Any movement which becomes successful goes through a series of troughs and crests before it finally reaches its apex. The only thing to be careful about in case of a people's movement is that it can't stay in a trough for long, because before you know it, it might just bury itself there. Time at that point was ticking for us, but then something happened and it completely changed the mood that evening,' reminisced Master.

Though the movement started off on a great note it couldn't continue its rhythm beyond a couple of days. The facts, figures, arguments and counter-arguments had become repetitive and monotonous. The crowd that was listening to all the speeches started turning into a noisy distracted lot. However, just then a vintage open jeep stormed into the City Centre. The driver parked the jeep right behind the gathering of volunteers and heads turned around in inquisitiveness.

Unrecognizable from a distance, people saw four individuals, laden with accessories, endowed with shoulder-length hair. They got off the jeep and moved through the gathering towards the stage. It was not long before one of the four individuals, in his semiformal jeans minus any sort of extravagant frills, attracted a huge uproar as he walked through the crowd. This man was Jack and it was Nirvana at 30 which had come to support Master's movement.

Master got up from the mattress and moved forward to catch a glimpse of the men. He was pleasantly surprised to see Jack and his band members as they reached the centre of the stage. Some sections of the crowd knew Nirvana at 30 but by now large sections knew Goa's very own Jack.

Some knew him personally, some knew him as the genius who had hacked into Grinnel's database and some remembered the early morning, 'Hi! This is Goa's very own Jack'.

Master welcomed Jack and his band and introduced them to his team after which he quietly asked Jack, 'By the way, what are you doing here?'

'Master, you're fighting for Goa and so you can always count on Jack for any support,' said Jack, with a passion that always rose at any mention of Goa. With these words, he turned back and came to the fore to face the gathering. He received a rapturous reception as he grabbed the mike and began to speak in his trademark style from his RJ days.

'A very big Helloooo and good evening everyone. Goa...,' shouted out an exuberant Jack. 'This is Jack. Wow...I mean, I've been in Goa ever since I was born but I don't remember the last time I saw people come forward and assert themselves this way. This is fabulous,' Jack said, with an excitement that drew roaring applause from the gathering. 'Yes, you deserve this applause and Master, Goa needs individuals like you,' he continued.

'People usually condemn, intellectualize and do a truckload of bitching about the system and its policies but it takes a very special man to actually stand up and do something.'

The applause didn't stop and the crowd reveled in pride

at the fact that they were a part of something special.

'I stand here, ladies and gentlemen, and salute each one of you for showing the courage that only a true Goan can. You have shown that we are simple and peace-loving people but if ever our rights are infringed upon or opportunity denied to us, we will rise together. We will demand answers and we will fight for our rights because…it affects us.'

The crowd shouted "It affects us" in a resolute voice. The deafening sound of this declaration soon gave way to a strumming guitar and the famous vocals of Nirvana at 30 as they performed the song "It affects us".

At the Hall of Fame ceremony Master continued his vivid account of this landmark movement. The movement's success was widely publicized but since it was a regional issue, it didn't hold a very important place in the minds of people outside Goa. Learning of the nuts and bolts of this movement was a revelation for the crowd. Master continued, 'That day Goa and I woke up to another revelation. We always thought Jack was a fun and happy-go-lucky person who could brighten any gathering. But that day we saw a Jack who could also be extremely enlightening, informing and above all, inspiring.'

'We don't need appeasement measures from the government,' declared Jack. 'Neither are we going to buy the logic that a rise in commodity prices in a free market system has nothing to do with governance. It is gross economic mismanagement which has created a demand-supply mismatch and hence the rise in prices. I do appreciate the state government for not burdening its citizens with escalating taxes. However, in view of the rising inflation, we need the cabinet to pass a note in favour of a revision of the minimum wages in Goa. This measure might not be favourable to small businesses or established corporate houses who look for greater production at lower wages, but we don't want a Goa where we have double digit growth rates and also have families which can't afford a double meal,' he continued.

'Yes,' shouted the crowd in affirmation.

'When a man like Jack talks about inflation, minimum wages and governance it is taken more seriously. That moment something just changed and for the first time I could actually sense the common man connect to the movement, something which had been eluding us. Once that connect happened I knew it was going to be a homerun,' exclaimed Master, thumping his hand on the table with excitement.

Jack departed the next morning with Nirvana at 30. They had done their bit and left the City Centre with a bang.

The movement by now was beginning to assume unprecedented proportions. The turnout was off the charts as people kept pouring in. Master immediately called up Edwards and apprised him of the proceedings. The entire team was now pressing for a response from the government. Vincent, in a fiery rhetoric, called out state representatives and demanded an answer.

Finishing his public addresss, Vincent came backstage and said to Master, 'We should get a response from the state in a day or two.'

'No…no…Vincent, we can't wait till then. The people who have gathered here might not wait till then,' asserted Master impatiently.

'Listen Siddharth, we're quite safe now. We have the support of the people,' Vincent said in his characteristic animated style.

Master quickly replied, 'Nothing is safe, Vincent. If there is something history has taught us, it is how vulnerable movements are when they're about to peak.' Master's pitch got louder as Mistry and Rishi joined the conversation.

Master continued, 'We are on a roll and the pace we have has to be maintained. These people need results or else their spirits will dampen. They have their lives to live, bills to pay, houses to run, kids to raise. They need only the faintest signs of futility and they will walk away before you know it.'

Everybody agreed with Master's argument and the next card out of their pack was Francis Edwards.

Edwards made his way into the City Centre without his ministerial paraphernalia and climbed the stage to address the gathering. It was supposed to be a rather important moment because for the first time a state representative was going to react.

Edwards in his modest attire stood behind the podium. His grey hair and heavy tinted glasses gave him further credibility. He took off his glasses, rubbed his eyes and spoke, 'I had a word with the Finance Minister and the Chief Minister. Unfortunately, the government has chosen not to budge from their stand.'

A huge uproar spread through the crowd.

'I, as the labour minister of Goa shall not accept this,' declared Edwards.

Amidst the deafening applause, Edwards spoke further, 'I declare to the state, "fire me if you want" but I'm standing here and supporting this cause because more than anything else—It affects us.'

The declaration resonated among the crowd and marked the beginning of serious inroads that Master and his team were making into the state machinery.

⁘

'It was game on from there onwards. A state minister siding with the movement was just the sort of shake up the government needed. As far as the movement was concerned history was in the making,' enthused Master. So strong was Master's narrative that the gathering at India Gate had by now started exuding the same kind of euphoria as the actual yesteryear gathering at Goa's City Centre was gripped with.

⁘

By the evening of day five the situation was such that news channels were covering each and every step of the movement. Edwards had completely taken over the centre stage and he didn't shy away from firing salvo after salvo at the state government. Vincent got a much needed respite and was now managing the operational part of the movement. And Master, the man had hardly put a step wrong. Every card he threw turned out to be a trump-card. Years of perseverance, diligence and experience were reflecting in every move he made, every decision he took and every word he uttered.

However, Master could now sense that it was time for the final dash towards the finish line. He immediately called for a conference backstage.

Addressing the meeting he said, 'Around an hour back, I received a call from the Chief Minister's office. They tried to persuade me to give up this movement. When I pushed our demand for labour revision, they continued beating around the bush.'

'The Chief Minister in a press release has unequivocally condemned our movement and has termed it undemocratic,' added Vincent.

'Our license for protesting at the City Centre expires in two days. The state might cite security as a concern and deny us the right to stage such protests,' Rishi added.

'Look, I see only one way out of this,' said Edwards.

'And what's that?' asked Master, as everybody turned towards Edwards.

'A state-wide labour strike,' declared Edwards with conviction.

The statement drew sharp responses from the entire group. Vincent got angry and said to Master, 'Siddharth, so far our movement has been lauded for its allegiance to peace and democracy. Tomorrow if we go on a strike, not only do we erode production output and set an example of bad economics, we also run the risk of being at the receiving end of law enforcers.'

Vincent's point had merit and no one countered it before Edwards responded, 'Vincent, you've been talking peace, diplomacy and protocol all this while. Has it gotten us anywhere?'

'What do you mean? You see the crowd standing outside? Doesn't that tell you a story, Edwards?' asked Vincent.

Master tried to intervene but no one listened and Vincent continued, 'Listen Edwards, for us a lot is on line. Do you get that?'

The tension between Edwards and Vincent was palpable as the other members including Master feared a major showdown. The remark didn't go very well with Edwards who sharply retorted, 'Oh, don't give me that Vincent, I just tossed out my ministerial portfolio so keep your "lot on the line" talks to yourself.'

Vincent was not a man who'd be bullied around and taken for a ride. He snapped back at Edwards and said, 'That's the problem with you people. You want brownie points for everything you do.' He was getting wicked and mean by every passing second.

Edwards was fuming with rage at Vincent's condescending remarks. The situation was delicate as Master tried helplessly to dissuade them. However, what followed was a string of verbal slander and the meeting derailed completely.

The situation was so combustible that Master chose to stay quiet and order for silence. After such a nasty fall out followed by a moment of awkward silence, Vincent stormed out of the meeting to grab a smoke. Edwards was more livid than anybody. Amidst such soaring mercury levels, even Mistry couldn't speak his mind.

A potent movement suddenly seemed like a ship without a rudder. It was tossing hither and thither at the mercy of winds.

The crowd outside was getting restless and so was the inquisitive paparazzi waiting for a fresh set of media bytes. Master was also jittery and undecided. He knew it would be only a matter of time before their indecisiveness became publicly apparent and the movement lost steam.

Rishi and the other juniors from Master's consultancy looked towards a rather disillusioned Master and pressed him to address the gathering.

Master took off his glasses and stood engrossed in introspection. His eyes feverishly looked everywhere in search of any suggestion. But there wasn't a semblance of it. But then, there was a reason why people called him Master. A couple of jittery steps soon gave way to his characteristic, majestic swagger as he stormed on to the stage. The crowd cheered loudly as he came on stage and it wasn't long before he was bombarded by a volley of questions from the media.

Master grabbed the microphone and walked from behind the podium to the centre of the stage.

'The state has responded. They want us to call off this movement immediately and in return they are assuring us that the best interests of Goa will be served,' stated Master.

The crowd at the City Centre was expressive enough to convey their negation straight away.

Master strolled around and sarcastically repeated their words, 'The best interests of Goa. Five sugar coated words which actually mean "screw you, we'll do whatever we want".'

Every word came out stronger than the previous one as Master's stirring address continued.

'So they are not going to listen to us. We have only one more day before our license to protest here expires. What do we do?' asked Master.

'Do we pack our bags, go back to work and pretend that this never really happened or take the fight to the next level?' Master asked the gathering.

The crowd passionately and unanimously shouted for the second option. They were not going anywhere without a fight.

'Thank you. You've made this much easier for me. One thing is clear—we will stand here and fight,' Master pronounced loudly. The applause echoed his resolve.

'But friends, today we are confronted with a challenge as to how we should take this movement forward. This forum has been privileged enough to have the company of some of the best minds in Goa. Vincent Nazareth, Francis Edwards, Mistry, they are all stalwarts and I'm honoured to have worked with them.

'Many of you might not know that, but Vincent and I go back a long way. I remember that the first time we met was when I was in college. I was young, restless and naive enough to question his acumen. As years passed, Vincent and I went from strength to strength and as I grew in this field, I realized why Vincent is what he is. The man can take criticism and move forward. It takes a very big heart, ladies and gentlemen, to put everything aside and work with minnows like me.'

Master's oratory and sheer warmth was top notch. Backstage every single word he was saying was being heard by Vincent who had lit his fifth consecutive cigarette.

'Today, standing at this crossroads, I feel that there is no one more eligible than this man to show us the path forward,' said Master.

Vincent was completely taken by surprise. He quickly stubbed out his cigarette and stood up, not knowing what to say. Now after five smokes, ten minutes of solitude and Master's resolute interaction with the gathering, Vincent indeed had made up his mind.

He called out everybody from the backstage. Edwards, Mistry, and the entire gang came out as Vincent then spoke emphatically

He came on to the stage and declared, 'Ladies and gentlemen, the entire labour force of Panjim and four other districts will go on strike from tomorrow.'

A murmur started in the crowd and media alike. Everybody was surprised at what they had just heard, especially Edwards.

Master smiled and gave Vincent a thumbs up as he spoke further. 'I know this is a tough call. Even I was rattled when I heard this but I looked around and saw you and all I could think of was the spirit to fight. I looked further and saw these young people (pointing to Rishi and other juniors) and I could sense a hunger.' He sighed for a second and then continued, 'I didn't stop there and looked around further and I saw Siddharth and all I could think of was Master.' Vincent warmly smiled as Master acknowledged his gesture. The crowd cheered for them in respect. 'Well, I'm not done yet. The last person I saw was Francis Edwards and all I could think of was selflessness.'

Edwards couldn't quite believe what he was hearing. But then that was Vincent. Just when you thought that he was egoistic and hot-headed, he would surprise you with his human side.

Vincent continued, 'A man who can throw away a cabinet post for his conviction has to be of a twenty-four carat quality, ladies and gentlemen. I am not a goldsmith but this man is pure gold.'

Everybody on stage and backstage clapped louder than the crowd. The ice had been broken and a consensus had been reached.

'Now let's talk business. As I said, we're giving the state government twenty-four hours. Either they pass a cabinet note for a revision of the labour wage or we go on strike starting from Panaji to the rest of Goa,' declared Vincent.

The movement soon took a serious and sensitive turn on its last day. The protesters' license was to expire in a few hours. The representatives of the state government had gone hammer and tongs criticizing Master and his team's method of holding the state ransom. They didn't budge and on the contrary, they suggested severe action in case the protest turned violent. Mistry, Vincent and Edwards meanwhile, hadn't even rested their backs over the last twenty-four hours. Years of experience handling labour and unions had helped them ensure that the daily wage workforce from all four districts was on the same page standing together in protest at the City Centre. The place became more inflammable when security guards and police forces took positions and surrounded the area.

'I don't think it is a good idea to have common people here anymore. They've done their bit. All we need here now is the labour force,' said Master to the entire team gathered backstage.

'I second that,' said Vincent.

'We have to be quick because in an hour from now things could turn chaotic and we don't want to give these so-called law enforcers any chances,' cautioned Edwards.

Master nodded in affirmation and promptly called out to the juniors, 'Listen everyone, you take your positions and when I give the signal ensure the smooth exodus of the people present.'

Master with Vincent and Edwards went to the main stage. Without wasting any time he addressed the gathering.

'Friends, it's time when all of us want to thank each one of you. We salute everyone present here and the one thing we can ensure right now is that all of us are going to make these seven days count. For now, we are continuing this fight with the aggrieved labour force of Goa. It is important that you now head back to your homes and support us from there. Kindly ensure you don't create any chaos and exit peacefully,' requested Master.

With these words, Master and his team galvanized into action and started helping the people find their way out. Master's volunteers were doing a fine job managing the crowd. The labour force that was to continue the agitation had assembled in one corner and from the other end people were leaving the City Centre in large numbers. Everything was proceeding smoothly when suddenly things began heating up at one of the exits. It was one of the points where civilians, the police force, the labour force and all media persons were present.

Loud slogans from the labourers fuelled the already heated atmosphere. A couple of police officers reacted sharply to the slogans. The people making their way out also echoed the slogans. Edwards could sense some tension and he ran towards the spot to avoid any possible confrontation. Before Edwards could get to the spot an aggressive police officer came forward and forcefully pushed the labourers.

'Keep it down, I say,' shouted the police officer, as he shoved a couple of protestants. Rishi didn't take that very well and shouted in the man's defense, 'Officer, you have no right to touch him.'

That statement irked the officer and he ferociously rebutted, 'Shut your mouth or else tell me, I'll do it for you.' A few more heated words were exchanged and before anyone could react, the officer pushed him down to the floor.

Edwards reached and tried to intervene, but it was too late. The crowd took offence at the officer's actions and retaliated.

The place was so cramped that it was only a matter of seconds before a small scuffle boomeranged into an ugly war.

Master and Vincent could see everything crumbling in front of their eyes. He and Vincent shouted over the microphone in a bid to pacify the crowd. However, the situation went out of hand and turned into a violent slugfest. The police suddenly went berserk and what followed was a mindless lathi charge.

Amidst the furore Master saw a man lying in a corner in a pool of his own blood. It was Edwards. A wild swinging lathi had busted his nose open. The pushing and nudging soon snow-balled into a stampede. Vincent lost his temper and shouted at the officers before he was pushed aside and rescued by other members of his team.

The violence at the City Centre had turned into breaking news across all channels. Sharp reactions started pouring in from all quarters. More than a dozen people, including a couple of journalists, were seriously injured and the situation was in complete disarray.

The police was absolutely relentless and the worst part was when they opened water shells at Master and his team. Master cried for help for an injured Edwards. The situation was turning ugly and Master knew that he had to keep his cool. Drenched in water, he stood up and stealthily sneaked out of the chaos. Master's glasses had been broken. The banners, the makeshift stage, the sound system and other paraphernalia were all damaged. But what wasn't damaged was Goa's will to fight for this cause. Master knew that fire for fire would not be the right move. He composed himself and called for an ambulance. Meanwhile, Rishi had managed to help Edwards to his feet.

Master's eyes were desperately searching for Mistry. He found him slugging it out with a police officer in one corner.

Master immediately reached for him and pulled him to a corner.

He hurriedly said to Mistry, 'Listen carefully. Edwards is hurt. Rishi is taking him to the hospital and you have to take command here.'

Mistry hastily asked, 'Where are you going?'

Master yelled, as it was difficult to hear in the chaos, 'We don't have time, Mistry. Vincent and I are surrendering to the police. You carry on the movement along with the labour force. This incident will fan a lot of emotions of the labour class across Goa. Get them on board.'

Mistry heard him out before their dialogue was rudely interrupted by a massive push that nearly knocked them to the floor. Separated by a couple of feet and half a dozen people, they did exchange a final few words, 'Mistry, it's in your hands now. Take this movement to the finish line, brother. Just do it.' With these words, Master rushed out of the chaos and went straight to the main stage. He met Vincent and an unstated mutual understanding between the two prompted them to surrender to the police immediately.

The police had by then brutalized a large number of people, from civilians to Master's team to the media.

There was not a single section of the society that didn't take notice of this and launch a scathing criticism. The media took them by their necks. Running footage of Edwards' condition and the mishandling of journalists fuelled the angst of the people. All sorts of conspiracy theories were discussed. Ministers, industrialists, everyone was in the dock. However, the issue found its true calling when it resonated across the floor of the state assembly. This issue came as a welcome opportunity for a starving opposition. A huge outcry in the house compounded by comprehensive media coverage pulverized the state government into submission.

Vincent and Master had struck a homerun by surrendering to the police and getting arrested. Hundreds gathered outside the jail. Mistry had done an exceptional job in building a consensus amongst the labour class and organizing a march from the jail to the State Assembly. It was a master-stroke which stoked sentiment and drew massive support from the masses and the media alike. Three police officers were suspended with immediate effect. A deeper investigation by the media threw light on a potential police-state-industrial nexus behind the sabotage.

.11.

I High-fived It with My Heart

It was 3 a.m. in the morning when an exhausted Jack entered his home. Ever since Samantha had left, Jack barely came home. He walked straight to the living room and then reached over to the closet where all his mementos were kept. There was a gigantic hacker key, a jockey megaphone and now a new entrant was a dummy microphone inscribed with the words 'Nirvana at 30–Jack (Banjara)'.

Jack had quit Nirvana at 30 that night. Like every time, there was no particular reason why he had quit. He just knew he was done rocking and singing.

As he placed his memento in the closet his already clouded mind started getting flooded with memories of Samantha. She hadn't responded to any of his messages over the last three-four days.

This was killing Jack. He picked up his phone and called her up at four in the morning. The call did go through as Jack, who was in a different space altogether, began pouring his heart out.

'Sam…Sam…how is your side of the world?' asked Jack.

Sam could sense the slur in his speech and despair in his tone. She didn't, however, react and said, 'You know what time it is, Jack?'

'Oh, I know. It's a tough time, Sam. I'm aware,' replied Jack.

Sam sighed for a second and said, 'Jack, I heard about you dropping out of Nirvana at 30.'

'Awww...alright...alright,' said Jack with exuberance.

'What?' asked Sam.

'You still keep a tab of what your hubby is doing?' teased Jack.

'Oh...yes, I can't stay away even for a second,' said Sam, sarcastically.

'I know sweetie... I know that,' said Jack with laughter that exuded more pain than joy.

It was followed by a few moments of silence after which Sam said, 'You're losing it.'

'Don't worry, honey. It's only after losing that one realizes what winning is,' came Jack's reply.

'Uh...you can't change, can you?' asked Sam, rather irritated.

'Now you can't accuse me of that. I have changed. I was a hacker, then an RJ, then a Rockstar...,' Jack continued before he was interrupted by Sam.

'Oh...please...Jack...,' shouted Sam.

'What? See, I've changed. You tell me who your favourite Jack was?' he asked.

Sam paused for a second and said, 'It was the Jack I met. The one who showed Goa and life like never before.' Barely able to hold back her tears she said in a husky voice, 'Because after all Goa is the second best sight on Earth.'

Jack smiled and completed the sentence, 'Yeah, right. Because the best sight is Goa with Jack.'

The two shared a brief moment of laughter and love. It was soon after suppressed by an unstated awkwardness which Jack had earlier mentioned on his radio show. But certain instincts didn't stay suppressed after that conversation. In fact they came out of the closet and meandered through the streets of Goa.

˜

'Young lady, we're standing right next to Miramar beach. This place is special not just for its picturesque location but also because years back a very handsome young man found his lady love right here,' Jack, the travel guide, informed the lady.

This travel guide had a tale of his own romanticism with the city for every tourist spot. He knew Goa, or should we say Goa knew him.

It was only a matter of time before 'Goa with Jack' became a buzz word throughout the city.

Jack didn't just show people the Goa they read about in books or heard about from friends, he made them smell the essence and feel the spirit of Goa. There was hardly a nook or corner of the city where someone or the other didn't have a personal equation with him.

Cookies at Mr D'More's place and margaritas with good old Joseph had become a norm for every visitor. Jack would make sure every tourist took a slice of Goa's life back with him/her.

One evening, after finishing his regimen with the tourists, Jack stayed back at Joseph's place. He was in a pensive mood, lying down on the beach and staring at the waves as the evening paved way for what was going to be a long and thoughtful night.

Joseph could tell that something wasn't right. He got a few drinks, some prawns and home-cooked steak to accompany them for the night.

Placing his companions by his side, Joseph asked, 'What is wrong, Jack? Are you meditating?'

Jack despondently laughed, 'Sometimes I wish I had that

level of focus.'

Joseph laughed and said, 'But then you wouldn't be Jack anymore.'

Jack replied, 'Yeah…right but what good is this Jack for. You know what, Joseph? There comes a time when more than experiencing things, you want to fulfill them. You want to make a difference.'

Joseph placed his hand on Jack's shoulder and said, 'Jack, you are a rare talent and you know that. There is no one I know who can spread happiness and joy the way you can.'

Jack impatiently replied, 'I disagree. I couldn't keep Sam happy. She doesn't love me anymore. Her parents hate me. Where am I spreading this love and happiness you talk about?'

Joseph laughed. He had never seen Jack so negative and insecure about himself.

He said, 'Who told you they don't love you? Trust me, they can't live without you for long. It's just that they can't accept the fact that one man can be so outrageously convinced about the way he lives his life.'

'I don't know Joseph. Earlier I never asked myself where I was going, why I was doing something or what I was really up to? But now these questions have begun confronting me,' expressed Jack.

'Jack, why did you quit hacking?' asked Joseph.

'I don't know for sure and I didn't ever bother to analyse it but I guess it wasn't exciting anymore and I wasn't good beyond a point and…,' Jack paused for a while.

'And…?' asked Joseph.

'I didn't quite like the concept of intruding into Goa's privacy. Moreover, I was also blocking Rehan, who looked like he would make a good manager. It's all complicated. I don't know,' said Jack.

'And the RJ bit? Why did you quit that?' asked Joseph, as if trying to get some point across.

Jack thought for a while looking for a concrete answer. Struggling with "Ahs" and "Ohs" he finally said, 'I can't say. I would be lying if I said it ceased to excite me. It did but then I thought, maybe we could have some awareness or social programme for Goa on that slot. And I thought the new show *Goa matters*, would perhaps be better than the one I was doing.'

Joseph immediately asked, 'And what about that rock band? You loved singing and playing the guitar right from your college days. What was the reason there?'

Jack was silent for a while. 'Now don't say that it didn't excite you. Nirvana at 30, sellout crowds, girls going crazy, who would leave all that?' asked Joseph.

Jack thought for a bit and replied, 'It wasn't doing anyone any good, was it? It didn't matter. It didn't affect the lives of people here. Barring the "It affects us" movement where it brought people together, it didn't do anything more than entertain them.'

'Exactly. You nailed it!' Joseph continued. 'It didn't do anymore. Yes, it didn't really matter beyond a point. The fact is that you want to do something or make way for something that matters to people, that matters to Goa.'

Jack listened carefully to Joseph who continued, 'Every time you quit, you might not know it but subconsciously you have a reason. The reason is not your clichéd, 'I don't get a high anymore' but that you never hang in there for the heck of it.' Joseph's pitch rose over the last words as he continued digging deeper to drive home his point.

'You are a giver, Jack. You have always wanted to contribute to Goa. This is not a new thing that you are saying today. The fact that you want to contribute rather than just experience has always been true. It's just that now you are beginning to realize it, kid.'

Joseph's voice and lips were trembling with conviction and purpose. Jack was perplexed by Joseph's analysis, who then smiled and said, 'Just hang in there, kid. Keep following your heart and one day you will know your true calling.'

Joseph's assuring smile and hand on Jack's hair cheered him up as he reciprocated with a wink and said, 'True calling… Ha…did I ever tell you about a Czech girlfriend I had named, True?'

Joseph was glad to finally hear some vintage Jack-esque anecdotes.

Over the next few days, Jack continued having fun and so did the visiting tourists. Nothing had drastically changed about Jack, except that now there was a purpose in everything he did.

Goa with Jack included amazing races, Jack's personal trysts with the city, home-cooked steak and new untapped facets of tourism.

He explored greater dimensions of Goa. There was a lot more to Goa than just beaches, sunsets and picturesque postcards. Medical tourism and biotech tourism were unheard terms with regards to Goa's tourism portal. However, Jack took it upon himself to put these on the map.

It was Jack who used his 'Goa with Jack' clout to meet with officials of the tourism ministry. They discussed at length various ways by which tourism, the staple source of Goa's revenue, could be given a fresh impetus in a time when recession and security concerns were rather potent deterrents. In a presentation to the tourism ministry, Jack eloquently articulated a possible opportunity for alternative forms of tourism in Goa.

'Sir, Goa's tourism proceeds contribute to 10 per cent of the state's revenue. It employs 12 per cent of the State's citizens and God knows what other great things it does. But there is also another side to it,' said Jack.

'Nobody says it but tourism also dents certain aspects. Like the fact that there is a water shortage in the market areas,' pointed out Jack.

'The water problem is turning acute, courtesy the hotels which have been taking away most of the water to meet the tourist demands. The same goes for power,' reasoned Jack.

The ministry officials heard him patiently and saw merit in what he said.

'This brings me to the fact that with growing tourism, let's not just bring in windfall revenue or jobs. There is lot more that we can do,' assured Jack, as he took them through his presentation.

'Healthcare is one sector which is showing great promise here in Goa. And that's precisely why I see a very strong case for medical tourism. Gentlemen, if you run through some facts pertaining to the healthcare system in Europe, you will find that for simple procedural operations they have to wait as long as six to eight months. That's a huge time lapse giving us a great opportunity we can cash in on,' said Jack.

'We could come up with plans promoting medical treatment in Goa plus an additional recovery holiday package as an incentive,' reasoned Jack.

Jack knew the pulse of the city and its people and was bubbling with ideas that could push the envelope for the state's already flourishing tourism department.

After a few more meetings and some rigorous hours of brainstorming, they were all sold on some of Jack's innovative ideas, ushering in a wave of alternative tourism.

Alternative seemed to be the buzz word in Goa. Some prefixed it with tourism, others with government and still others with labour wages.

Post the arrest of Master, the "It affects us" movement had caught the fancy of almost every Goan. With a state assembly held to ransom by the opposition, an industrial sector crippled by labour strikes and a police setup at the receiving end of persistent flak, the state government was gasping for breath. The noose was further tightened around its neck by Mistry, whose ground skills of labour unification and strategic mobilization, suffocated their last chances at negotiating or striking deals.

Master's statements from jail further upped the ante. The one thing he was grossly concerned about was his family's well-being. Master by now had become a controversial figure who had staunch critics and adversaries from amongst the political clan and corporate circles. Master was playing with fire. Sakshi and Master's parents visited him in jail and apprised him of the world outside. They had been going through a plethora of emotions from despair to concern to satisfaction and above all, pride.

With a silent prayer in their hearts, they all came back home wishing that all this would soon be over. It seemed like the authorities had heard them that night because the next day an all-party meeting was announced in the state assembly. A session was finally called and the sole agenda of the house was labour wage revision. After eight hours of mind-boggling arguments, counter-arguments, verbal slander, insinuations and what not…a consensus was reached.

⁂

'Read my lips, ladies and gentlemen…I remember each word that was said back then. The state government has cleared a cabinet note for 7.5 per cent hike in the minimum wages for Goa.'

Complete euphoria broke through the crowd at India Gate. After an absorbing two-hour narrative, they knew what those words meant to the man sitting in front of them.

⁂

The battle was won, the mission accomplished. The countdown for Master and Vincent's release had begun. They had already received the good news the previous evening and the night before that was the longest night of their lives. The next morning, on 15th July, thousands of people gathered outside the jail to welcome their leaders.

⁂

Master was absolutely silent for a moment. The man just wanted to bask in the cherished memory of that moment. Clearing his throat he said, 'A lot of people ask me what winning is? Is there anything like winning in the first place? That Sunday morning I touched victory. I felt it with my hands, saw it with my eyes and high-fived it with my heart.' Master's excitement was so infectious that hardly anyone in the crowd could sit.

'Phew….and after an hour or so, for the first time since the movement started, I felt tired. I just wanted to go back home and bury myself in my bed for good. I wanted to sleep as if

there was no tomorrow,' he smiled.

Well, if sleeping blissfully is what Master was indulging in, there was one guy who was busy waking up both himself and others to what truly Goa is.

'You know, Goa is also a hot bed for the concept of wellness,' stated Jack.

'Wellness?' enquired a tourist.

'Oh yes…you know spas, yoga, Ayurveda. It's another experience, you see,' articulated Jack as he guided the tourists to a wellness centre situated on top of a hill overlooking a picturesque beach and the sea.

The footfalls to wellness parks across Goa increased manifold over the next few months and so did the scope of medical tourism in Goa.

There was not a single aesthetic detail of Goa that could miss Jack's roving eye, seeking mysticism and belonging. His frequent meetings with tourism officials and the fact that 'Goa with Jack' had now assumed the status of a brand had given Jack a fresh lease of life.

He was breathing Goa and in the next few months he explored the nuts and bolts of the state.

From a romanticizing wanderer to an exploring tourist guide, Jack's relationship with Goa was evolving unlike the other cherished relationship that he had. It had been close to six months and Sam had shown no signs of reconciliation. A call here and a text there was all that was left of their relationship.

Sam's fashion designing career also found a new high in Mumbai. An otherwise optimistic Jack had now begun losing hope of things ever going back to normal. Ego, infidelity, aggression; none of these clichés had ever troubled this relationship which had slowly run out of steam for no specific reason. Setting everything aside, Jack did make another valiant attempt to salvage his relationship. He went to Mumbai to attend Sam's fashion show.

It was an upmarket Bandra fashion show where Sam's range of gowns was on display. On display, however, were also Jack's emotions and intentions to reconcile with his wife. Backstage, Sam was busy dotting the "I"s and crossing the "t"s when Jack sneaked in and greeted her with a rather buoyant, 'Hi!'

Sam responded rather quietly without making eye contact. Jack's smile was trying hard to hang around but it was only a matter of time before it gave way to a grin and then a disappointed look.

Sam was coordinating with one of her crew members when Jack interrupted and said, 'We need to talk.'

Sam, however, stayed busy with her piece of cloth and didn't bother looking towards him as he stood next to her.

'Tell me, Jack,' she replied, trying to appear unfazed.

'Sam, what do you really want?' asked Jack, in a straightforward manner sans any antics or light banter.

'Does it really matter, Jack?' she asked him, nonchalantly.

'Of course it matters. Sam, you're my wife. You're the best thing I have ever had. How can it not matter?'

'Wow…the award for another round of sugar-coated verbosity goes to Jack,' she replied, rather sarcastically.

A usually calm and smiling Jack was beginning to lose his cool as Sam continued to ignore him. He turned hysterical. He snatched away the piece of cloth in her hand and said, 'Listen to me when I speak.'

Sam was irate and in a fit of rage she pushed him aside,

'Stop it. If you can't focus on one thing, at least let others do it.'

The echo of that sentence was loud enough to rattle the people around them, who either moved away or chose to ignore it.

Jack hadn't expected such a sharp reply from Sam and was taken by surprise. He didn't say a word after that. The silence of a man who wears his heart on his sleeve is an alarming sight.

Sam kept working on the piece of cloth in her hand. A cursory look at her effort with the cloth showed quite clearly that it was not what she was concentrating on.

Jack started walking to the door when Sam called out to him, 'Jack….'

Jack stopped as Sam asked with bated breath, 'Is it all over?' Sam's voice was laced with pain and anguish. Tears were knocking hard on the doors of her eyelids.

Jack thought for a second, turned around and said, 'Sam, between you and me, it can never be over.' 'Never ever be over,' he stressed.

.12.

This Is My Yard!

'I raise a toast to Master's Consultancy Pvt Ltd. It has been a record-breaking year,' said a jubilated Rishi.

Everybody around him joined in the celebrations at a suburban hotel in Mumbai. Master and Sakshi gracefully attended to the guests. Leading industrialists, heavyweight politicians and the ever-so-omnipresent bureaucrats had all turned up to congratulate Master on the stupendous success his consultancy had received ever since they had shifted base to Mumbai.

Post the success of the 'It affects us' movement, Master had become a famous figure. Business opportunities had drawn him to Mumbai and what followed was a barrage of offers, collaborations and strategic alliances. The celebration party today was a PR exercise to send the people of Mumbai a loud and clear message that Master had arrived.

Mumbai had been very kind to Master and his family and slowly they cemented their place in the financial capital of the country. Goa was now reduced to a branch office which Master seldom visited.

His close nuclei remained almost the same. Retired from politics, Edwards was now working as a full-time activist. Vincent, however, now worked as a freelance advisor to the Finance Ministry in Goa. Besides this, he had also become a partner in Master's firm. Mistry, the man who had actually taken Master's movement to the finish line was now in the reckoning to be the next labour minister.

They were all present at the party, catching up with each other, remembering their old days of struggle.

'Master, there is one thing you have got to admit. If anyone amongst us has benefitted the most from this movement it is you,' claimed Mistry, gulping down his fourth drink.

Master laughed and helped himself to some snacks.

'And what about you, Mistry? You're in contention to be the labour minister. Who could have imagined that?' asked Vincent.

'Though the ruling party in Goa, the People's Republican Party, has been kind to me, nothing is confirmed yet,' Mistry replied.

'Isn't it a shame, Mistry?' quipped Edwards. Continuing, he said, 'They were the ones who did everything they could to sabotage us and today you are ready to join them at the first sign of something lucrative.'

'That's not how I see it, Edwards. I see them as the ones who eventually did pass the cabinet bill and revised labour prices,' stated Mistry.

'But not before they resorted to lathi charges, water shell firing and everything they could to crush us. Not before they were cornered on all sides by everyone, from the media to the opposition, to the citizens,' elaborated Master.

'They didn't pass the bill...Goa forced them to, Mistry,' he clarified.

Mistry laughed and said, 'You sound like one of those leaders from the opposition party, the Goa Democratic Front, who keep saying the same thing.'

Master immediately replied, 'Guess what? I met their party president, Mr Menezes, at a function here. He looks promising.'

'Yes, their prospects look good for the Lok Sabha polls and Menezes is a gem,' said Vincent, as these old pals bonded over cocktails, politics and gossip.

'I agree with you. The anti-incumbency is also huge this time. But in Goa it is the candidate and not the party that the electorate gives a mandate to,' stated Edwards.

Master yawned and stretching himself, said, 'God bless Goa!' as the discussion moved to other topics and people.

'How is it going with your friend, Jack?' asked Mistry, helping himself to a muffin, as Sakshi also joined the conversation and made sure Mistry had his plate full.

'He is sort of disconnected,' replied Master. 'I left a message but haven't heard from him. When I heard of him last he had become a famous tourist guide,' said Master.

'Goa with Jack. I read about it in the papers,' said Sakshi, rather indulgently.

'He is a misguided missile, I tell you. A waste of life,' Vincent said mockingly and rather dismissively.

Master laughed and said, 'Vincent, you know, ever since the success of our movement, lots of questions and "what if this", "what if that" have been doing the rounds in my mind. The one question that always comes up is that on 15th of May, the second day of the movement, what would've happened had the "misguided missile" you just mentioned not landed at the City Centre?' asked Master.

For a moment there was an introspective silence but then Vincent said, 'Come on, Siddharth. That's giving him way too much credit.'

'I am not giving him credit. But the day this so called

misguided missile gets its true calling, it will be unstoppable. And I have a gut feeling that day shall come soon,' stated Master.

Vincent carefully heard him and said, 'Phew...' After a second, in a light vein he shouted, 'Because it affects us...!'

Everybody laughed. His timing was perfect and the flood of memories it brought was so huge that for the next five minutes the laughter did not die down.

Meanwhile, the misguided missile had stopped again for a refill. It had toured and criss-crossed every nook and corner of Goa. From implementing landmark tourist suggestions to absorbing the essence of the city to having cherished moments of fun and laughter with tourists, Jack knew it was time for 'Goa with Jack' to call it a day. But this time there was a difference. 'Goa with Jack' had ceased to excite him. But he was not done with Goa.

He wanted to stand in the centre of the city every day, feel the pulse of the city and do something but he wasn't clear what that something was.

'The misguided missile, ladies and gentlemen, was hovering around Goa with a compass-needle tossing hither and thither refusing to stop and point in one direction. All he did know was that no matter where the compass needle pointed in the end, Goa would be the common denominator,' said Master with a smile. Clearing his throat, Master said, 'This common denominator would continue to fascinate Jack. The difference was that the avatar had now changed. If the tourist Jack was a complete sell-out, then the new avatar "Citizen Jack" was a blockbuster.'

Citizen Jack—two words which would go on to stir the conscience of Goa. Goa's very own Jack had now donned the hat of a citizen with a conscience. A citizen who would mirror the grit, triumphs and spirit of the city. A catharsis of his experiences, his trysts with the troughs and crests of the city formed the basis of a daily column, *Citizen Jack*, published in Goa's largest read tribune.

If Goa with Jack gave newer dimensions to tourism, *Citizen Jack* took government accountability and citizen activism to a completely different level. Jack's column addressed *Citizen Jack* in the third person. His penetrative eyes exposed incompetent government authorities, sluggish officials and unnoticed yet significant problems. It didn't stop there. He also officially registered complaints, looked for action and found heroes amongst common citizens who facilitated good for Goa at large. The column was laced with angst, emotion, spirit and at times even dollops of humour, driving the point home.

Jack had now started living a pretty secretive life. He would never be seen in parties or social gatherings and this greatly helped his purpose.

As far as his fellow Goans were concerned, they had lost count of his different avatars. The bottom line was that they never ceased to get enough of him.

Citizen Jack took a quantum leap when it boomeranged into a full-blown television production which aired every Sunday morning across regional television channels.

"Citizen Jack has gone satellite", was the headline in newspapers across Goa.

In Jack's words, 'I had never thought that one day I would

be on television. Not that I had thought of being on the radio either, but this was very unexpected. However, I wasn't excited at all. Maybe because I was too focused on the job at hand or maybe because things had now ceased to excite me, as much as they seemed to ignite me.'

The first episode of *Citizen Jack* was a highly anticipated one. Rumour had it that some high profile person would be part of the inaugural episode and face the music. The stage was set for Jack, who was a bag of nerves. His RJ experience did come in handy but facing the camera and keeping the audience engaged was a challenge for him. The format of the show was a unique one. Each episode would have its first half dedicated to an existing issue prevalent in Goa. This would comprise an expose on the incompetence or the foul play of authorities, if any, and would also seek pragmatic solutions to the same. The second half would be an in-studio shoot where Jack would have a tete-a-tete with either some distinguished individuals from Goa or with unsung local heroes.

'The inaugural episode of "Citizen Jack" was very special. It was the first time anybody had ever heard of a newspaper column getting adapted into a TV show. For Jack, it was not just a quest to know whether he could pull this off or not, it was something he had started developing a very deep passion for. As far as I am concerned well, it turns out that "Citizen Jack" was equally special for me,' said Master.

With minimal make-up applied and a collar mike firmly planted on his black overcoat, Jack sat cross-legged on an old couch in the green room. He was minutes away from going on air. The confident, suave Jack that the world knew was nowhere to be seen. The person who sat in the confines of that green room was the real Jack—someone who was nervous, probably for the first time in his life. He was insecure and apprehensive at attempting something new but above all, he was afraid of failure.

There was also a brief moment when Jack just wanted to escape from this reality. But the very next moment he anticipated the contentment that he would experience if he managed to pull it off. Every moment carried with it a different story, a different emotional graph, until the moment of truth arrived and Jack was given the final cue-thirty seconds to go.

A deep breath followed by a silent prayer and out came Jack—people's Jack, *Citizen Jack*. When the camera rolled, on display was the quintessential charmer Goa loved to fall prey to.

However, spreading charm wasn't his endeavor that day and one could sense that over the years, the charm Jack exuded as a radio jockey or a rockstar or a travel guide had now evolved into a poignant voice determined for change.

Jack's first words did indeed ring a bell, 'Ladies and gentlemen, boys and girls, children of all ages. A big hello and a very good morning from Goa's very own Jack!'

'Now many people have asked me what exactly this show is about. Will it be similar to the friendly radio show *Jack's thy Answer*? Or will it just be a montage of exposes and issues we all know about but care little for. Well, as far as *Citizen Jack* is concerned, it will be a lot more than this. Our endeavour is not to create a ruckus but to seek a solution. One such individual who is testimony to this core belief of our initiative is amongst us today. He is Goa's very own and it's ironic that years ago this man was my guest on my radio show and today he's here as my first guest on *Citizen Jack*,' smiled Jack.

The studio audience cheered and started chanting Master's name.

'So, should we welcome him?' asked Jack.

'Yes,' shouted the audience.

'Ah...not so soon...before that we have some other people waiting. So let us welcome them first.'

The lights dimmed and the spotlight shifted to the entrance curtain.

And then the unexpected happened. A strumming guitar, a beat of the drums and out came three of Jack's old buddies, one of whom was crooning the yesteryear song "It affects us". It was Nirvana at 30 and seeing them reunite with their old buddy Jack got the audience euphoric. There were hugs, there were high-fives and above all, there was a raw pulsating spirit which would come out of the TV set and grip everyone in its sweep.

The microphone kept changing hands as everybody, including Jack, crooned the number "It affects us", which served as a symbolic prelude to Master's entrance.

'Ladies and gentlemen, the man who made Goa realize that it affects us. Please welcome, Master,' Jack called out.

Master's entrance received a huge applause and before any of the viewers realized it, they were completely absorbed in the show. Jack and Master were together on one stage on one show and they just carried on from where they had left off. What followed was one of the liveliest, most engaging and enlightening discussions Goa had had in recent times.

'So, Master, how has it been off late? We do keep hearing about your off the hook, and may I say, staggering success in the corporate world,' said Jack with an excitement that showed clearly how proud he was of him as a friend and as a fellow Goan.

'Thanks, Jack. Corporate success eluded me for a long time but thank God, it has come eventually,' Master said.

'It has indeed. Multi-million deals, acquisitions, forging powerful strategic alliances...you are on a roll,' claimed Jack.

'I can say God has been kind,' accepted Master.

'Goa is very proud of you and trust me, you are someone we all look up to,' said Jack.

Master nodded in acceptance and the studio applause did the rest.

'Which brings me to my next question, Siddharth. Where does Goa figure in your scheme of things today?' asked Jack, in a rather direct manner.

'I am glad you asked me this. Goa is an integral part of my plan and by the end of the show, I have an important announcement to make in this regard,' replied Master.

'The man who got us out to streets, who had the state government down on its knees, suddenly left the state just when it seemed like he was in the best position to make a difference?' asked Jack.

Maybe it was the direct nature of the question or perhaps it was the fact that he wasn't expecting Jack to be that probing, Master was caught unawares.

'Jack, I didn't walk out. My career started in Goa as a welfare economist. The "It affects us" movement will always be the watershed moment of my career. It made me who and what I am. I love this place and owe my success to it. But I see no harm in exploring and exercising new perspectives in Mumbai,' replied Master.

'Fair enough. But Master, trust me, Goa misses you. We

miss the man who has always kept his convictions ahead of any market norm or conventional belief that confronted him,' pointed out Jack.

'Well, since you have been missing me and vice versa, let me just cut to the chase and make my announcement. I have been thinking long and hard. Staying away from Goa wasn't easy but now the wait is over. Goa goes for the Lok Sabha elections this November and today on this platform of *Citizen Jack*, I, Siddharth Rane, officially announce my candidature for the Goa Democratic Front.'

It was a startling revelation, something neither the studio audience nor Jack had any idea of. It took them a moment to absorb the news and then applause followed as they wished him luck and support.

'I must confess that I didn't see this coming,' smiled Jack, as he extended his hand to congratulate Master.

The discussion went back and forth as Jack tried his best to get a fair idea of Master's vision for Goa.

He pointed out, 'The Goa Democratic Front hasn't really done much with regards to critical issues and neither do they boast of an impressive governance record. The fact that they have been sitting in the opposition for such a long time stands testimony to this.'

'Well, from where I see it, they have encouraged investment in the state. Goa today needs a progressive government,' said Master, with conviction.

'Well, if a progressive and development-oriented government is what Goa needs then I am afraid we already have one in power, going by your own words,' rebutted Jack, pointing out the particular date and context in which Master had called the ruling government a progressive one.

'The Republican Party is indeed progressive but none of their development plans have been inclusive in nature. I have said it in the past and I reiterate that I envision a Goa where every section gets what it deserves and every section is deserving enough,' laid out Master.

'I agree but you must understand that the problem with Goa is not its development. This is already one of the most self-sufficient and fairly well-developed states in the country. The problem is governance. The problems are local operational issues, something which was missing in your party's approach,' pointed out Jack.

Master's expression showed that he didn't like Jack's overt probing. Nevertheless, he stayed calm and replied, 'Jack, that's a thing of the past. We are starting afresh, and honestly, I have always adopted a macro approach. If you get basic parameters like investment, division of labour and resources right, then good governance shall follow.'

'I can't argue with an economist,' Jack laughed, making things a little lighter. Master also shared in the laughter and *Citizen Jack* wrapped up its maiden episode.

After pack-up Jack asked Master, 'Man, when did you decide to enter politics?'

'It happened gradually. Mr Menezes became a close friend and one thing led to another, so here I am. But what was up with you today? You were really grilling me about everything. You seemed to have lost it,' he said, while plugging out his ear phones.

'Come on, Siddharth. What I asked was basic and I didn't know you would suddenly drop the nomination bombshell,' replied Jack.

Master laughed and said, 'Anyway, what do you make of

it, Jack?'

Jack smiled and said, 'You remember my views on your first research paper?'

Surprised, Master tried to recollect.

After a brief moment he said, 'Yes…I do…'

'Well, I still don't think economists make good politicians,' came Jack's reply.

Master didn't exactly like Jack's view but call it grace or his first lesson in politics, he didn't let it show. With a smile on his face he said, 'Sakshi was thinking of you. Come home some day.'

Jack in his tongue-in cheek manner replied, 'Oh would have loved to but then you live in a different city these days.'

Master sportingly took Jack's dig in his stride and said, 'Not too far is it, not for a wanderer like you.'

Jack also took it sportingly as the two chatted away to glory for another hour, catching up on everything from Master's child to how Joseph was doing, to Jack and Sam's strained marriage.

While parting Master said, 'It keeps getting bigger and bigger every time we meet, Jack. First the movement, now my big announcement and your TV show. I wonder what's next.'

'Let us just hope it doesn't stop there. Our next meeting should be as big as Mt. Everest,' Jack winked.

Back at India Gate, Master smiled, remembering that day.

'Who could have thought that in two months Jack's prophecy would indeed come true…'

Amidst media coverage and buzz, Master's SUV vroomed into the office of the Goa's election commissioner. With three months to go for the polls, Master had come to file his nomination papers for the North Goa constituency. Accompanying him was the party president, Mr Menezes, who most political pundits thought had got a gold mine in the form of Master. Standing at over 6 feet tall, dressed in a traditional silk kurta with a waistcoat, Master cut quite a handsome and seasoned figure. His light framed spectacles and assuring smile did the rest as he waved to the media and entered the office with his entourage. He was so confident in his dialogue with the media that one could already see him as the M.P. from that region. Election campaigns, counting of votes and the actual result all seemed like a mere formality.

Political pundits and commentators claimed that North Goa was Master's yard and no one could stand against him.

Vincent, Sakshi, Master's parents and Mr Menezes were all present at the press conference rooting for Master. With élan, they presented their manifesto and vision document titled, *Goa 2.0*.

Purists lauded it as a progressive, development-oriented approach. There was also a section which panned it as a far-fetched and over-ambitious fantasy. But that didn't matter. With anti-incumbency riding high and a credible face like Master at the forefront, manifestos, campaigns and political opinions seemed trivial.

However, one man or rather one citizen, had by now carved a niche for himself by raising seemingly trivial issues and emphasizing their gross significance. *Citizen Jack* was in its eighth running week and in these weeks it had raised hopes, expectations, citizen awareness and of course, the TRPs of the

Sunday morning slot of the channel. The show was so well received that it received a special mention on the floor of the state assembly. Critics hailed it as a scorcher of a show and even though it had seemed commercially non-viable at one-point, it had garnered decent numbers and sponsors.

While on an outdoor shoot for the ninth episode, the production assistant, Raghav, asked Jack, 'Every week we come here and unearth issues, create attractive promos, talk to people, make them think for a minute and then pretty much move on, right?'

Jack sat on a wooden slab at the City Centre roadside where they were shooting and after thinking for a moment he replied, 'You are missing the point here, Raghav. The fact is that we are keeping the system on its toes. That is precisely what the job of the media should be. I am not a full-time journalist but trust me, *Citizen Jack* has become quite a deterrent to sluggish governance, at least for the municipal corporation. Over the course of the show so far I have filed more than a dozen RTIs and a couple of PILs.'

Raghav laughed and said, 'You've been quite a thorn in their flesh.'

Jack high-fived him and said, 'You bet your ass, I am...'

He continued, 'That's what we need. Citizen activism. Citizens who would go out there and demand an answer, who question what's wrong and above all, have a conscience. *Citizen Jack* is all of this.

'You are quite a seller, Jack,' quipped Raghav.

'Now that's one thing I haven't done yet. I would make a good salesman. What say?' Jack asked.

'Don't tell me that's what you are going to do,' said a worried-looking Raghav.

Jack paused for a while and said, 'No, just kidding. Let's get on with the shoot. I am really excited and looking forward to the response for this week's episode.'

'Me too. Exploring the night life and party scene in Goa against the backdrop of rampant drug usage and peddling should make for a very interesting narrative,' he said.

'Also, we are getting four to five individuals who are now completely rehabilitated from drug addiction. They will share their stories and in a tie-up with our sponsor, we are setting up a free rehabilitation centre on the outskirts of the city,' informed Jack.

'The shot is ready,' informed a crew member as Jack and Raghav got up and moved towards the heart of the market where the shot was setup.

While walking through the market, Raghav asked Jack, 'Jack, this drug peddling episode hits the bull's eye. How many more of these do you have up your sleeve?'

Jack smiled and said, 'I don't quite know. Every week I go out on the streets and just start exploring from the vigil eye of a citizen. Whatever moves me or stirs me is pretty much there on Sunday morning.'

Raghav gave him a thumbs up and proceeded to take the shot. Jack, like every other week, sank his teeth deep into the issue on hand.

As weeks passed, Jack's caravan kept moving. From drug peddling to tourist security to illegal mining, Jack had covered all fronts albeit one, which lay cold and untouched—his personal front. Sam's absence had left an eternal void in his heart, home and life.

The rare calls and messages had also stopped. The writing was on the wall. The hustle and bustle of the day's work would camouflage Jack's despair but it was only a matter of time before it started making deep inroads into his psyche. As if this was not enough, there came a moment that couldn't have been more ill-timed.

.13.

The Bugles Had Been Blown

There came a moment when Citizen Jack's vigil eye started acting strange all of a sudden. Like the spokes of a wheel, its vision pointed in all directions. A strange restlessness had gripped him and his otherwise sharp eye failed to focus and capture anything. Jack's roving eye galloped through the streets, marched over the highways and meandered across the beaches. It seemed as if the entire state of Goa was gravitating towards his wandering eye. What was it? Was it his strained marriage playing on his mind or was it the fact that Citizen Jack had now run out of steam or maybe Jack had so much to tell that he couldn't quite pigeonhole it in a 30-minutes slot. Whatever the answer, it was all too clouded for Jack.

Contrary to his roving eye, was a very focused and pin-pointed vision aimed straight at the heart of Goa's political power. This vision emanated from Mumbai where the visionary, along with his close aides was busy brain storming his electoral strategy.

'Vincent, I don't quite understand why Mistry is so peeved with me?' wondered Master.

'Fine, he belongs to the rival party but we go back a long way,' he continued.

'Welcome to the world of politics, Siddharth,' replied Vincent, rubbing off his cigarette on the ashtray. 'Don't let this bother you. Once you are in power they will all become your brothers again,' he laughed.

'That's how fickle and opportunistic this place is,' he said.

After thinking for a while Master said, 'Vincent, I'm not too sure about how much time I would be able to devote to our consultancy post this. This has been worrying me.'

'There is no reason to worry. You have structured the organization pretty well and we have a decent team which can take care of it. Plus I will also keep an eye. And Siddharth, you are just going to Goa. I mean, how far is Goa from this place,' Vincent replied.

As the two continued their conversation, Rishi entered along with a senior party representative. Both, Master's Consultancy and the Goa Democratic Front were working closely on the poll strategy. Rishi laid out the map before Siddharth and Vincent and just when he was about to elaborate on the campaigning itinerary, Master stopped him and said, 'Let's wait for Mr Menezes. He'll be joining us in a while.'

Master did a brief pep talk with Rishi for greater responsibilities in the organization as they waited for Menezes.

A few minutes later, Menezes arrived along with his support staff. After the customary greetings it was business all the way for these heavyweights.

Menezes was otherwise an extremely assertive and demanding taskmaster. However, reckoning Master's stature, he didn't throw his weight around. Moreover, he completely trusted Master's acumen. Master, meanwhile, was of the view that he would keep the campaigning subtle and minimal. A research conducted by his team suggested that Master's image carried a mystique and an enigma which shouldn't be subjected to overexposure.

The discussion continued as everyone shared their views on the various opportunities and threats.

Menezes pointed out, 'Listen, Master, I firmly believe that you should kick-start your campaign from the City Centre. The "It affects us" connect that the place has would be a symbolic gesture to start off with.'

Master nodded and said, 'That's fine with me but I think it's time we moved beyond "It affects us".'

'Don't even think about it, Siddharth,' Vincent intervened.

'You mention Siddharth Rane to any person in Goa and chances are that his first words would either be "Master" or "It affects us",' stated Vincent.

'He is right, Master,' seconded Menezes. He then clarified, 'You see every politician and every leader needs a hook. We all crave for one. In my case, it is my surname, my family legacy. For some it is their ethnicity, their caste or sub-caste. For you, Master, that hook is—It affects us.'

Lending him a patient ear, Master registered every word Menezes said.

'Hmmm…right…but do you know who's standing up against me from the Republican Party?' asked Master.

'They haven't announced yet,' Menezes replied with a smile. 'That's the dig I took on them at my conference yesterday,' he informed.

Vincent laughed and said, 'Yes, I heard that one.'

He continued, 'The Republican Party is indecisive about everything from tax-cuts to mining licenses to labour wages. They are even indecisive about their candidate.'

The brainstorming continued back and forth late into the evening and inside that room right there was a happy unit basking in the glory of scripting a battle they knew was in their pocket.

The glory of a political entity is somewhere compensated by the agony of another. Such are the vagaries of politics. If the Goa Democratic Front was riding high on Master's credibility the incumbent Republican Party was having sleepless nights. Their incumbent M.P. Bhaskar Lobo had been painted as a local villain. Lobo had passed one harsh statement too many about Master, his team and the people gathered during the "It affects us" movement. The party had been in damage control mode since then. Despite their best efforts and PR machinery working overtime, Lobo seemed unlikely to cut ice with the electorate.

Whatever little remained of Lobo's goodwill was shredded to pieces by the relentless assault on his governance by Citizen Jack. Jack never resorted to name-calling. However the exposes and the constant questions raised on authorities had done their bit to dent the incumbent government's image.

They did, however, very soon heave a huge sigh of relief when a perennial thorn in their flesh, suddenly eased its way out. Citizen Jack had just walked past his final checkpoint. 'One more lap' was the unanimous request from sponsors and channel producers but Jack had now decided to hang up his 'Citizen' boots.

His last day at work this time was rather a quiet one. He had been very reticent and seemed withdrawn since the past few days.

The man who could effortlessly cheer up any person and any situation had become totally listless. It was one of those moments for Jack, when almost everything around ceased to intrigue him. With every passing hour and every passing day, Jack was sinking into a quicksand of anxiety and self-doubt. The once carefree explorer now preferred to remain confined to the four walls of his apartment.

More than anything else, he was missing Samantha. The prospect of losing her had started dawning on his mind. He felt helpless, confused and for the first time in life, he felt that he had lost control over his life.

The crowd at India Gate listened in stunned silence. Never had they been that serious and that disturbed during Master's entire narrative that day. The silence was a testament to the love and concern people had developed for Jack.

'Jack looked a mere shadow of his prime. He seemed done and dusted. He began questioning his very convictions. Every single decision that he had taken, every move he ever made, was now under his own scrutiny. It was very unlike the man who would look the devil in the eye and say—this is my moment and I am not looking back or forward.'

'Phew…,' sighed Master as he paused for a while to clear his throat and have some water. The audience, meanwhile, couldn't wait for him to keep his glass down and tell them what happened next to Jack.

They anxiously waited in silence as Master resumed his narration with a teasing intrigue, 'And then came a phone call which changed everything.'

It was a quiet Saturday evening and Jack was munching some prawns and lazily browsing through TV channels when his phone rang. It was from an unknown number so Jack chose to ignore it. However, the calls didn't stop and so Jack finally did answer the phone. Nobody could have guessed who the caller was. It was A.N. Mistry, Master's close aide and former head of the labour union of Goa who shared the dais with Jack during the "It affects us" movement. He had barely interacted with Jack but today all of a sudden, out of nowhere, he emerged and wanted to meet him urgently.

Jack was initially apprehensive but he finally agreed to meet him at his office in Panjim. He didn't have a clue as to why Mistry, who probably was just an acquaintance, would want to meet him.

Jack entered his office and greeted him as the two sat down for a long hard talk. Jack saw a framed photo of him, Master, Edwards and some others standing hand in hand in support of the "It affects us" movement placed on his desk. He took the photo-frame in his hand, smiled and said, 'What a time that was!'

'Certainly. For some it was truly a time whose benefits they still continue to reap,' remarked Mistry.

Jack smiled and carefully heard him out. 'Think about it, Jack. This movement actually did give some sapping careers the kick they wanted.'

'Can't deny that and by the way congratulations on becoming the Labour Minister of Goa. Now that's what you call a kick,' winked Jack.

'Thanks Jack, but it is not going to last long, I reckon,' he said in a dismal tone.

Jack nodded and replied, 'With Master in the fray, quite honestly, there is very little you guys can do.'

'You think he will win?' asked Mistry.

'You think the sun will rise from the east tomorrow?' asked Jack.

Mistry smiled and acknowledged his answer. He pondered

for a while and said, 'Come Jack, come out with me.'

'Where?' asked Jack, in surprise.

'Just outside. I need to show you something,' he said.

Jack had been very surprised all along by Mistry's actions. He, however, followed him as the two came out on the street outside the office of the labour ministry.

'Mistry, what is it that you want to show me?' asked Jack.

'We'll have to walk down a bit for it,' replied Mistry.

Jack reluctantly agreed as the two leisurely walked along the street talking some random stuff which didn't have much of Jack's attention who was clueless about where he was going.

'It has been a while since I met Master,' said Mistry.

'Hey...,' Jack waved to an admirer who recognized him from the TV show.

Replying to Mistry he said, 'I can understand that. You guys are now political rivals.'

'I met Master around three months back for my show,' he told Mistry.

'Oh, I saw that. You're not doing it now, are you?' asked Mistry.

'No. I kind of...' Before Jack could complete his sentence, he was mobbed by a group of youngsters hanging around at a close by roadside restaurant. He cordially greeted them and also met the manager of the restaurant who offered him and Mistry a complimentary drink.

'This restaurant used to be a key tourist spot during my 'Goa with Jack' days,' remembered Jack.

A few blocks down, Jack and Mistry passed the street next to Grinnel's. Around a dozen hostellers who were near the marketplace for the weekly supplies immediately recognized Jack.

Before they knew it, Jack's news spread like wildfire in Grinnel's and soon dozens of students crowded the small market area.

This sort of reception and warmth came as a much needed breather for Jack who, since quite some time, had cocooned himself. It took about an hour for Jack to get over them and resume his chat with Mistry. He said, 'Come on Mistry, cut the chase and tell me what you want to show me.'

Mistry smiled and said, 'Turn around, Jack.'

Jack turned around and saw dozens of people who had lined up to catch his glimpse or have a word with him. He, however, couldn't quite gauge what Mistry meant to say.

Mistry continued, 'Jack, hear me out loud and clear...'

He looked Jack in the eye and said, 'Jack, do you want to be the next Member of Parliament from the North Goa constituency?'

Jack's ears couldn't believe what he just heard. His eyes couldn't dare to dream and his mind perhaps couldn't visualize what Mistry had just uttered. Cold-footed, he stood there numb for a few seconds as he suddenly felt an adrenaline-rush that would put to shame all other exhilarations he had ever experienced before. Incapacitated by the rush, he sat down on the road and slipped into contemplation. He somewhere saw this as a huge compliment to his body of work. There was pride, there was anxiety and there was a strange kind of euphoria.

As moments passed, Jack's instant euphoria slowly made way for self-doubt and insecurity that had cemented its place in his mind for quite some time.

'What do you say, Jack?' asked Mistry.

Jack composed himself and replied, 'Thanks a lot Mistry,

but quite frankly my answer is no.'

Mistry pressed him further, 'Come on, Jack. Look at these people. They love you. They want you. Goa wants you.'

'If there is anyone who can look Master in the eye and tell him that this is not his yard, it's you. Don't chicken out, Jack. You have never done that,' said Mistry, trying his best to pump up Jack.

'No. Mistry, I don't think I am capable of this and I don't quite believe in your party's ideology,' Jack clarified.

'Ah, chuck the ideological crap, Jack. The fact is that you are nervous, which I completely understand. Take your time,' Mistry replied.

'My answer will always be a "No", Mistry,' Jack said.

'We'll meet again…take care,' said Mistry as he shook his hand and took leave.

Jack quietly started walking towards the nearby bus depot. There was a stoic silence in his every action. Not that he was rethinking his decision, it was just that he was emotionally very drained out. His emotional wear and tear continued as he pondered over a countless number of things during his journey back home. His mind was restless and a throbbing depression continued to pulverize him. He wanted to talk it out with someone. A dozen names propped up in his mind but none appropriate enough to share his state of mind with. Fact was, Jack wanted to speak to Samantha. As the bus took the last turn approaching close to his house, he feared the prospect of going back to his lonely home. Call it coincidence or call it the power of the universe, Jack saw Samantha standing outside their home.

This day continued to amaze Jack. Perhaps it had taken a leaf out of his book and made him taste his own medicine.

He almost jumped out of the bus and ran towards her. He couldn't believe his eyes. He was so overwhelmed that when he came face-to-face with her, he just broke down. Samantha also couldn't hold back her tears as they hugged each other tightly.

Crying like a little baby, Jack said, 'You are not going anywhere now. I'll not let you go. I'll live like a hermit if you want. I'll be a fisherman if you want that but just don't leave me.' Jack blabbered in panic with tears rolling down his eyes.

Samantha wiped off his tears and reassured him, 'I am not going anywhere. Don't worry, Jack.' She affectionately cajoled him to calm down.

Jack had become so vulnerable and insecure that he refused to let go Samatha from his embrace.

'Jack, I'm not going,' said Samantha. Coming out of the embrace, Jack sat down at the gate of the house.

'Jack, please come inside. I need to speak to you,' she said.

Jack got up and the two entered the house. To Jack's surprise, Sam had already been there since evening.

'Sam, I missed you and I am never letting you go again,' assured Jack.

'Honey, I missed you too. That's why I'm here,' she replied, holding his hands.

'And you are going to stay here now,' said Jack.

Sam warmly smiled and nodded her head.

'No...no...say that,' he said.

'Alright sweetie. I'm here and I'll stay here...happy?' she asked.

Jack was still breathing heavily as the two shared a warm moment, which had been eluding them for quite some time. Jack was so exhausted that he fell asleep in her lap as she kept ruffling his hair gently. Finally came some peace for Jack who had all day been an emotional wreck.

As far as Sam was concerned, it was difficult to gauge whether her arrival that night was a one off visit or a permanent one. However, by the look of the two, they seemed to be doing pretty well, until a couple of days later when Sam took a message on Jack's behalf. The caller happened to be A.N. Mistry.

Just when Sam thought Jack had turned a new leaf and was done with experimenting, the bombshell of his tryst with politics dropped.

Jack got petrified at the prospect of Sam knowing about Mistry's offer. He immediately got in damage control mode and said, 'Honey, don't get mad at me. It is just a stupid offer I declined.'

Sam was slightly puzzled as she asked, 'What exactly was his offer, Jack?'

'Well, he had this far-stretched fantasy booking for me as their candidate for the upcoming polls. Can you beat that?' said Jack.

Sam was trying to connect the dots between what she could gather from Mistry's message and what Jack was telling her.

'Honey, you have my word here. I'm done being stupid. Not any more am I going to bite more than I can chew and neither am I going to make those valiant attempts to pull-off things,' clarified Jack.

Sam's expression of bewilderment and contemplation rattled off Jack who feared she being mad at him again. He sat next to her and putting his arm round her shoulder tried to explain, 'Trust me this time.'

Sam didn't reply and went outside to the lawn. Jack stayed back and wondered how peeved Sam was. For the next few minutes, a nervous Jack kept trying to assess Sam's mood.

His wait was finally over when Sam called him outside.

As Jack went outside, Sam said, 'Come here, Jack. I need to speak to you.'

Seated right next to her on a small fence, Jack waited for her to speak.

Sam cleared her throat and said, 'Do you remember the day we eloped and got married?'

'Sweetie, that's the number one with a bullet on my billboard list of achievements,' winked Jack.

Sam replied with a straight-face, 'No, Jack. That's not the point.' Sam was getting a tinge emotional with every passing minute as she continued, 'That minute, that second when I came out of the gate, I saw something that told me that I can't let him go.'

Jack patiently heard every word as she said, 'That something was belief. I believed you. Even if you didn't say a word, it was there in your eyes that you love me and I have never doubted that.' Jack warmly smiled on hearing this.

'You may sound naive, but I do believe you,' she said. 'I believe you, Jack,' she said with an élan.

'And you know what? The people too believe in you. When Citizen Jack tells Goa that they need better health care, we believe you. When a stupid RJ tells us that you should always tell your loved ones how much you love them, then like it or not we go out and do that. That's what you are, Jack.'

'You may have been confused but your belief has never staggered. Jack, I left you not because I stopped believing in you but because your belief is too damn strong,' she asserted.

'Never let this belief go because ten years ago the Jack I married was all belief. Today, the Jack Goa swears by is nothing but this belief?' Sam smiled as she affectionately caressed Jack's face. Jack was so taken aback by the moment that he couldn't react.

She held his hand and said, 'Now listen to me carefully. All your life if ever there has been a thing which has fired your imagination or got you out of your chair, it's Goa. You breathe this city, Jack. I know it since we met the first time. It's in your eyes, Jack.'

'Goa with Jack, *Citizen Jack*, *Jack's thy Answer*…I can bet my last flying buck that nobody knows the place, the people, the terrain better than my husband and I am proud of it. And you know what? More than me, Goa is proud of you. The people of Goa believe in you. They believe in the man who reaffirmed "It affects us". They believe in the citizen who worked his butt off to improve the system.'

'Phew…they believe in the Jack whose heart beats for Goa and who knows what it takes to make it better. It has always been a bond between you and Goa and today destiny is giving you this opportunity to do more for this city.'

'Everything you ever did, every friend you ever made, every moment you ever shared with anyone, it all gravitates down to this and you can't be turning around and saying no today.' Samantha said.

Jack was absolutely zapped. He was too overwhelmed to speak. 'But Sam, I can't be doing this. I don't think, I have it in me to take on such a big responsibility. Moreover, the Republican Party and I don't quite agree on a lot of things,' he said.

'Jack, since when, did you ever need anyone to tell you whether you have it or not. You're the man who has always taken it chest on and pulled it off, more often than not…,' she said.

'Yeah, but this isn't about pulling it off. Is it?' asked Jack.

'Trust me. When it comes to standing with the people on the ground and solving their problem, you'll not pull it off. You'll nail it...,' she asserted.

Jack remained quiet for a while and so did Sam. She then gently ruffled his hair and in a very relaxed and calm tone said, 'Sweetie, I'll tell you something that I learnt from you. Just shun the world outside and look within. You'll hear a thousand voices screaming and one-by-one, you'll see all of them die down, except for one and that'll be the voice of your beating heart. Listen to it, Jack and you'll get the answer.'

The drums started beating. The symphony swelled up like a tsunami and Jack was indeed hearing a thousand voices—voices from his past, voices from friends, from Grinnel's, from the radio station, from the tourism ministry, the channel headquarters, newspaper editors—voices from everywhere. All of a sudden Jack felt so much energy in him that he put on his shoes and went for a run. He could see his entire life flashing before his eyes. From the random jokes in the Grinnel's corridor to the serious chat with Joseph. From dropping out of Grinnel's to standing on the "It affects us" podium and addressing thousands of people. From the roving eye that wanted to capture the whole of Goa to the visual where dozens were waiting outside Mistry's office to catch his glimpse. He just kept running but finally stopped in front of Mistry's office.

The visuals had also stopped and the voices inside the head too faded out with every passing second. He could just see one visual in front of him—that of the whole state of Goa gravitating towards his eye. This time it made perfect sense. It had been in the making all this while and that precisely was the sentiment his beating heart echoed to him.

From a bundle of nerves till some time back to a pure adrenaline driven go-getter, Jack entered Mistry's office. He was breathing heavy and sweating profusely. It took him a minute to calm down after which he entered his cabin. Mistry stood there in anticipation and welcomed him.

Jack went straight to him and tightly hugged him. Mistry wasn't expecting this gesture. However, he complacently smiled and was quite relaxed to see Jack by his side.

'Mistry, thank you so much,' he said.

'It's okay, Jack. This is just the beginning. We'll go places.'

Jack held his hand and said, 'Pardon me, Mistry but I can't accept your offer.'

'What are you saying Jack?' asked a rather puzzled Mistry.

Jack replied, 'I don't know what is in store for me. I have no clue whether I will succeed tomorrow or not, but whatever may be the outcome, I'll always be grateful to you for showing me that visual outside Grinnel's.'

Mistry was still quite dumb founded at what Jack was saying.

'Had it not been for you, Mistry I would have never known that I have it in me to even think about contesting for the election,' said Jack with gratitude so deep that even his firmly rooted passion seemed pale in comparison.

'But you just refused my offer,' said Mistry.

Jack apologetically said, 'Mistry, I can't be competing on the Republican Party ticket. If there is one thing I have it is my belief and I am really sorry but I don't believe in the Republican Party.'

Mistry found that offensive and rudely asked Jack, 'So who else is giving you a ticket?'

Jack smiled and said, 'I don't need one. I am going

independent. Pretty much the way I've always gone about things.'

Mistry got infuriated and said, 'Jack, this is not about strumming a guitar or exposing an official. Do you understand that? You go independent today and you'll be lost in the ocean of anonymity like a dozen others.'

'Mistry, I can't be more lost than I was. From here it can only be up the highway,' said Jack with a pleasant smile.

Mistry was completely rattled and by the look of his expression, he wanted Jack out of that place as soon as possible. He made no bones about it and turned his back to attend to something else.

Jack decided to leave, however just when he was about to exit, something struck him and he came back running.

He went and hugged Mistry and said, 'Mate, I'm sorry. Forgive me, if possible…'

With these words, Jack signed off or should we say signed in for the biggest battle of his life.

Back at India Gate there was a volcano waiting to erupt as Master spoke, 'Ladies and gentlemen, it was going to be Jack vs Master.' The crowd erupted with joy and anticipation.

He continued, 'It was his flamboyance vs my fortitude. It was his mementos vs my trophies, it was "I pulled it off" vs "It affects us", it was moments vs legacy.'

The chants kept getting louder. It was madness there at the India Gate. They weren't gonna stop. This story of Jack and Master had just transcended the levels of mystic romanticism. Master was all smiles watching people in front of him go completely bananas. He tried to speak but every time he came near the mike, all he could do was smile at his helplessness. Sakshi, Vincent, Mistry were all elated to see the humongous public reaction.

Finally, as some sanity returned in the gathering, Master came back on the microphone and said, 'The next day Jack filed his nomination papers. The battle lines had been drawn. The bugles had been blown and I had never been so pumped up to win something all over again.'

Master's expression of the enthusiasm and the ruthless competitiveness that he possessed at that time was palpable to the audience as they waited for the finale of this saga.

.14.

This Is Our Everest!

The next day, Goa woke up to a familiar voice.

'Ladies and gentlemen, boys and girls and children of all ages…this is Jack and Goa, well, we're back together. We can't stay away, can we?' spoke Jack to a thunderous response from everyone gathered at the convention centre.

'You know, I've been a lucky chap all my life. I've received so much love from you that, honestly, I can never pay you back. No matter what I've done, you've always been there for me.'

Jack announced with a sense of gratitude, 'Today I stand before you Goa and promise you that from this day onwards, every ounce of sweat, every drop of blood and every beat of my heart is for you.'

The applause kept getting louder. He continued, 'Over the next few weeks I'll try and give you reason to support me for the upcoming elections. I don't have a political party backing me and neither do I have a corpus fund to support my large-scale campaigns. Quite frankly, I don't need them. All I look for is your support and your belief in me.'

Jack continued to enthrall people as he declared out loud 'I am independent. And that's how I want my Goa to be— Independent, prosperous and efficient. Thank you and God bless you all.'

As soon as he completed his addressal he was bombarded

with a volley of questions by the media.

'Jack, how do you fancy your chances against your friend Master and how will it affect your personal equation with him?' asked a media person.

Jack smiled and replied, 'I've been a huge admirer of Master and I came out in his support during the "It affects us" movement. I feel, it will take a lot to better him but if this place is his yard, it's also my playground. And as far as our equation goes, it dates back to our college days and I don't see that changing anyhow.'

'Jack, you got to be living in Lala land to think you can stand against Master,' a journalist remarked, condescendingly.

Jack's smile however didn't leave him. 'You're right. I am living in Lala land called Goa. That is the kind of Goa I envision where even an independent man on the street without any Godfather or any setup can dream of making it big on the sheer basis of merit. That's the Lala land I dream of, mate,' replied Jack in his charismatic style.

If he was spreading his charm and trying to prove to Goa that he's fit to stand toe to toe with Master, his rival on the other hand was being convinced about the contrary.

'What made him think that he's even your league?' asked Vincent in a dismissive way as he put down the regional daily whose headline read 'Jack vs Master'.

Master didn't react to Vincent's statement and continued reading the excerpts of Jack's interview in the newspaper.

Vincent mockingly laughed and said, 'Master, why don't you give him a call and tell him not to make a fool of himself at such a level. You are his friend and if he is being a jerk you should caution him. That is what friends do,' he argued.

While Vincent's rant against Jack continued, Menezes

entered looking quite calm and relaxed.

He informed them, 'Everybody, we have the press waiting outside and by the way, Master, your rally at the City Centre was off the hook. Great Job. We are planning another one there in the coming weeks. I'll also accompany you this time.'

Vincent sharply reacted, 'We would not need one, Menezes. Our victory would be long sealed before that. If you go by our model, it's sealed even if none of us move our butts from today.'

'What model?' asked Menezes as he checked the mail kept on his desk.

'Master didn't tell you about our recursive-predictive model which we've been working on for years?' asked Vincent.

'No,' Menezes replied.

'Well, it's a software-driven economics model which takes into account different parameters and can predict the results of the polls with near-about perfect accuracy,' he said.

'That's the advantage of having an economist on board. They'll always be ready with numbers,' he laughed.

All through this conversation Master was drowned into various editorials and journals.

Menezes worriedly asked him, 'Master, is anything bothering you?'

Master nodded in disagreement, though his pensive look spoke otherwise. Getting up from his recliner, he asked Menezes to accompany him outside for the press conference.

Out came Master with his team and then what started was a verbal slugfest that didn't end right till the election day.

On being asked about the possible threat from Jack, Master took a royal dig on his old friend. He smiled and said, 'Which Jack are you talking about? I know a lot of Jacks actually. One is a guitarist, one is a TV show host and there are half a dozen others as well.'

Everybody around had a laugh as he continued, 'Seems like he has got his finger in too many pies and I am afraid, Goa is not a pie you just taste and move on. Talking of pies, I think he should try being a chef as well.'

'What? Has he done that already?' Master inquired.

Master's dig at Jack, though friendly in nature was actually a deliberate and meticulous attempt. Menezes announced a rally near the convention centre on the coming Saturday. With spirits soaring high and an upbeat morale, Menezes left with Master and Vincent in his Ambassador. The car moved and he laughed and said to Master, 'Master, you really handled the Jack part well.'

Vincent, sitting in front sharply said, 'I don't think we should even mention him much in these press-meets. He is trivial.'

Master cleared his throat and said, 'Vincent, you remember the time you called Jack a misguided missile?'

'Oh yes, I do. I stand by it still,' he replied.

'Well, not any more Vincent. This missile just found it's true calling. Mark my words, he's coming at us and trust me when I say that this man will put in everything he has,' cautioned Master, with a straight face which for a moment bothered Menezes.

Menezes said, 'What makes you think that, Master? That man is just a vagabond. He has no party, no funds, nothing behind him. What does he have?'

'The people. He has the people behind him,' replied Master which completely silenced Menezes and Vincent.

It were the people indeed who accompanied Jack on the streets as he marched on to the local power station. Jack was all fired up against local power theft and so were his supporters as they barged into the office of the Power Commissioner. Jack was building momentum quite quickly. He got a petition signed by the local citizens and registered a complaint against power theft in the district court. Jack's campaign had hit the streets of the city. He didn't need any trumpet blowing sidekicks or craftily designed punch-lines and slogans. He was his own publicity.

If the issue of power theft rung a bell with the common people, then the issue of water crisis hit a homerun. Jack and his bandwagon entered the Water Authority. It was the issue Jack had raised at his show *Citizen Jack* as well. Jack approached the tourism ministry, where also he had been quite a figure during his tourist guide days. He was trying to get to the bottom of all these issues which affected the common man.

Jack's approach was hands on and rooted to the ground. It was just four weeks to go for the polls. Jack had by now started building quite a buzz which could be heard all over the city and even across the corridors of the Goa Democratic Front headquarters. The Goa Democratic Front was now waking up to the challenge. As far as Master was concerned, it rubbed him the wrong way and brought out his ruthless, competitive streak. At that juncture, Master played an absolute genius of a stroke, true to his name. He issued a formal challenge to Jack for an open debate. It didn't take much time for Jack to agree as he didn't have an option. However, deep down he knew what he was getting into.

'The local news channel TV Goa, stepped in to organize the debate between me and Jack. Looking back, I wish it had pan-

India coverage. Anyway, the stage was set and, what better venue for this other than our own Grinnel's,' remembered Master.

⁓

Grinnel's was ready and so were the students, for whom Jack and Master had by now become cult figures.

The main auditorium which had once been witness to Jack's 'Banjara Main' and Master's 'Gardener' speech was today going to host one of the most anticipated clashes. The build-up to this had started days in advance. Huge posters of the two and some archival tapes of their days in Grinnel's during the college fest and farewell had been doing the rounds on the giant projectors placed all across the college.

Joseph too chipped in with his anecdotes regarding the two. So many episodes, so many instances of Jack and Master had been tastefully narrated by Joseph that it would be fair to say that these two characters were still breathing alive in Grinnel's. Master, fresh from a road show drove straight to Grinnel's in his SUV. Giving him company was Sakshi, Vincent and a couple of party representatives. He was focused and intense. As he got down from the car, he was ushered in by the college dean and the representative from TV Goa. He and his entourage entered in the auditorium amidst huge cheer and claps by the students.

As Master was walking up the stage, he saw Joseph standing right there. Master respectfully greeted him and the two exchanged a warm moment. Everybody now waited for Jack to arrive. Their eyes were glued to the main gate. Ironically, years back, it was this college which showed him the gate. Little did it know, that one day it would open all gates and stand on tenterhooks for his arrival.

And then came Jack. The man didn't have a convoy of people with him. He didn't carry any baggage or frills. It was just him and his wife Samantha by his side.

There was not a single person there who didn't know the Jack-hack episode. For the geeky ones he was the man who hacked into Grinnel's website, for the chilled out clan he was the quintessential banjara, for the intellectual class he was Citizen Jack.

And there was one man for whom he was simply the young chap he knew right from the first day of college. That man was Joseph and when the two met, there was a huge cheer from the audience who knew about their special bond.

Everyone waited with bated breaths as anticipation rocketed through the roof. Though Jack appeared very calm, deep down the butterflies were going crazy.

The cameras rolled and the moderator who was the editor-in-chief of TV Goa took the centre stage.

Jack and Master, both came out on stage and greeted each other.

Jack smiled and quietly said, 'Master, this is our Everest.'

'As far as I'm concerned Jack, this is my yard,' Master replied in strong words as the first round of the debate kick-started.

Both of them were given ten minutes to spell out their vision of a better Goa and their own constituency.

Master started off eloquently and within a minute-and-a-half, he had everyone listening and breathing his vision. His vision was a structured model of how investment, fiscal deficit and better tax structures could be managed. Master's addressal touched upon the socio-economic issues and its biggest strength lay in the inclusive nature of his proposed

This Is Our Everest! • 215

reforms. The success of the "It affects us" movement further consolidated the belief that Master stood for everyone, right till the least denomination of the society. His famous baritone and commanding confidence was an absolute masterclass for the young students. Next up was Jack. There was a certain degree of reticence in Jack's body language. He had a shaky start where he did try to turn his charm on but was quick to realize that it alone won't keep him afloat. However, after an initial minute or two of uncertainty and apprehension, Jack did come into his groove.

Jack's addressal didn't have a very academic or scholarly approach. It was embellished with a ground-level citizen connect. Basic amenities and day-to-day issues topped his priority list. However, on the face of it, his vision lacked the sophistication and finesse that Master had. In a gathering of young economists and scholars, the weighing scales had already started tilting towards Master.

The next round was the crucial rebuttal round. Jack wasn't getting the energy from the crowd that he was used to. The smile didn't elude him but his confidence had begun to dwindle.

It was Master's turn to ask Jack some questions. 'Mr Jack, you mentioned a large number of issues from water crisis to quality of roads, education and even healthcare. How do you plan to rope in the investment to meet the increasing demand of these sectors?' asked Master.

Now it's not that Jack didn't know economics, but Master was playing to his strength today.

Jack cautiously started, 'It's a very good question but can't say how important. I'll come to its importance later. As far as your question goes, I feel the state government must issue bonds and financial securities especially for the infrastructure sector. That way we can raise money and generate a corpus fund to meet the state requirement.'

Master calmly smiled and said sarcastically, 'Now that's elementary economics revisited.' The gathering laughed out loud as Master continued trying his best to dig deeper, 'You see, Jack, such funds have been in place for the last decade and a half. You haven't told us anything new. Also a dozen such securities have come and not given the expected return to the shareholder. What different do you plan to do?'

Jack quite frankly didn't have any answer to this question. He did, however, try to put up a fight. 'Well, in that case I'll listen to what my financial secretary tells me.' He laughed and so did others.

'And I bet he will be some economist,' he laughed more. Master gently smiled, however in no way was he willing to let go of Jack without getting him to answer this one.

Jack did fumble around for a while and then said, 'You're right, Master. For a decade and a half such schemes have existed but what also existed all this while is decent investment in the state. It has never been a problem. It's one of the richest states of this country vis-a-vis its population.'

Out of nowhere Jack suddenly propped up a relevant argument which got him back some much needed confidence.

'Investment is not a problem in Goa, ladies and gentlemen. The problem arises when the MP development fund and the foreign investments are not used judiciously. Now that's what we call governance and not investment,' said a pumped-up Jack.

'And that's the explanation to why this question wasn't important. Thank you,' Jack clarified with authority. It did help him win some points in the last minutes but overall the first half of the debate belonged to Master.

Round two was a few minutes away as they went in to get a breather. Master's camp could smell victory. On the other side, Jack was a nervous wreck. 'Sam, am I making a fool of myself?' asked Jack rather frankly. Sam could sense that Jack was losing focus and belief.

She got up from her couch, held up Jack and said, 'Jack you're doing fine. The fact that you are standing there and everybody around is watching you means that you belong to this place. Believe in yourself honey and above all start believing that you can beat Master. You can beat that guy, standing there, Jack,' fired up Samantha.

'He doesn't know which road, which hospital or which reservoir of water in Goa needs attention. He can quote economics, investments, shares and a whole lot of bookish junk for all I care but he is not Goa's own Jack.'

Sam was desperate to somehow motivate Jack out of his shell.

It was time for the final round. The moderator asked Jack to question Master on whatever he wanted.

Master was ready and you could gauge that by his confident body language. The moderator said, 'Jack you can ask Master your question.'

Jack smiled and said, 'My question is not for Master. It is for Siddharth Rane.'

That statement elicited a lot of reactions from the audience. Some Master loyalists booed it, some casually had a good laugh and others just waited with bated breath to see where this was going. As for Jack it was high time he brushed aside the Master aura and looked him eye to eye.

'Siddharth, your fantasy Goa 2.0 manifesto mentions about

healthcare and identifying that as a problem it plans opening eighteen new centres right?' asked Jack.

'That's right we need more centres to meet the demands,' replied Master.

'How well you know what the problem is,' smiled Jack sarcastically.

'Siddharth the problem is not the number of centres, but the number of qualified doctors in each centre,' he stressed. 'There are dozens of centres around Panjim but the doctor-patient ratio is what the concern is. You walk into any centre... they're not overloaded. There are vacant beds lying with no doctors to attend but to know this Siddharth, you'll have to walk into one,' hit out Jack, who for the first time that evening seemed to be in control.

Master, however, laughed it off and said, 'That's what happens when you keep a very narrow perspective of things, Jack. The healthcare sector is growing at a double digit rate and courtesy the recent spurt in medical tourism, we need more centres. I guess you need to read about the tourism ministry's report on medical tourism.'

Jack smiled and said, 'Siddharth, you're talking to the guy who headed the committee on this report.'

'Woah' was the immediate chorus from the audience followed by thunderous claps all around and Jack seemed to be clawing back in the competition. That was Jack's standout moment of the day. Master missed out the point that it was Jack who during his tourist-guide days pioneered the cause of medical tourism.

Back and forth, the arguments continued.

'You talk about industrialization, Siddharth. Well, the areas you've marked out have major water issues. Also most of them are residential areas so the health hazards are huge. I wonder how beneficial such industrialization would be,' reasoned Jack.

It was down to who could tilt the debate towards his individual strength. After a couple of rare instances where Jack brought out local operational issues it was all Master. Master quite eloquently dismissed Jack's approach as too micro and too myopic to sustain the challenges ahead.

If Master was reiterating his creed about taking Goa to the next level, Goa 2.0, Jack's core ideologue was Goa Fine-tuned. Jack firmly believed that Goa, already being one of the most developed states, didn't need some magical plan or fantasy vision. All it needed was fine-tuned and well-balanced governance.

However, Jack's approach didn't cut much ice with the audience beyond a point.

Some of the verbatims coming from both ends were hilarious.

Jack took a royal dig at Master when he said, 'That problem there is visible. Yes, of course if you are sitting in Mumbai, then it may not.'

Master too didn't spare him when he said, 'For this sort of governance, you need a stable government backed individual and not some independent banjara.'

It soon came to an end as everybody anxiously awaited the mandate of the studio audience.

The studio audience voted 66 per cent to 34 per cent in favour of Master. A thumping victory of this sort did a world of good to Master and his team's morale. As for Jack, well, that was possibly the best he could have done.

Once the dust was settled and the two returned home, it was time for some serious introspection.

Master's camp though seemed pretty relaxed while driving back from the college.

Sitting next to Master in the backseat, Sakshi cheerfully said, 'It was after such a long time that I was seeing Jack and Samantha. They're a beautiful couple and Sam, she hasn't changed one bit over these years.'

'Yeah, right,' had been Siddharth's standard reply to everything Sakshi had said all through the journey.

'What happened, Siddharth? I mean you just had an amazing debate which you won hands down. What's worrying you?' she asked.

'Nothing really,' said Siddharth.

Vincent sharply reacted, 'Ah…come on Siddharth, you should not be breaking any sweat over this chap. Though I must confess, I was expecting even better than 66-34.'

Master replied, 'Vincent, the fact is that this person out there eats, sleeps and drinks Goa. He knows this place, he knows the issues and surely he knows the people out here.'

'I don't care a toss about how much Jack knows the place and its realities. Fact is this doesn't matter to the people. 66-34 today…come election day and it might be 80-20 or 75-25, if that punk's lucky enough,' said Vincent in a rather off-hand manner.

Sakshi further said, 'Siddharth, quite honestly Jack looked completely out of sorts today. I've been an admirer of his in the past but today he wasn't anywhere close to you and frankly after today's loss, I doubt he'll be able to muster any courage.'

Master smiled and said, 'Oh this man sure knows how to rise back. And he will, trust me. I know him damn too well. Sakshi, in the next two weeks he is going to put up a show like only he can.'

Showtime, indeed it was. The next day saw a resurgent Jack get up from his bed and hit it out in the centre. He was right there in the centre of his playground and he played with every ball, every goal post and every toy that was there. Jack had absolutely nothing to lose. He knew that in the form of Master, he was indeed stepping up against the absolute best and he would have to pull out everything he had. Early morning that day, Goa woke up to a yesteryear chant, 'Ladies and gentlemen, boys and girls…' and the rest was needless to utter as Goa's own Jack donned the RJ hat for a one-day-only episode of *Jack's thy Answer*. The nostalgia for Jack and the audiences alike was overwhelming. Everybody in the studio too was more than happy to have Jack back. As the ball got rolling one could see the yesteryear charm retained and strong as ever before. The amount of incoming calls clocked by the station in that one hour was unprecedented.

'Vote for Jack' was the buzz word in the radio headquarters as Jack invited everyone hearing him across the radio for a rally over the weekend.

However, the player wasn't done. Next up was another familiar place and familiar people. It was the reunion of Nirvana at 30. The crowd at Imperial Club was elated to see their yesteryear banjara. A couple of songs, a vote appeal and an invitation for the rally, the ball kept rolling.

It rolled all the way, through the streets of Goa right till the regional Goa TV headquarters and that evening at the prime time slot, the city saw the return of one of its prodigal citizens—Citizen Jack. The special episode of *Citizen Jack* was an absolute scorcher. Jack, in that episode, explained distinctly his vision for Goa, his identification of issues and above all the solutions he deemed fit for them.

The highlight of it was Jack spreading out the entire map of the constituency in front of the camera and talking about every ward, every street, their issues and challenges with utmost precision.

There in Master's camp, one had started feeling the tremors. The momentum Jack had built over the last week was beyond the buzz created by any PR agency driven, well-managed campaign.

With less than ten days to go, this battle was heating up.

Master, meanwhile, was focused and pretty strongly footed on his paved path. His pamphlets and manifestos were stuck across the walls of universities, corporate offices and the by-lanes of his constituency. Across events, conferences and press meets he was absolutely spot on and in sync with his plans.

During one of these meetings and constituency tours, he ran into an old friend and admirer Francis Edwards. Edwards had been nominated for the Magsaysay Award for his outstanding contribution to social services over the last few years. The two friends caught up over tea and what followed was some honest, straight forward heart-to-heart talk.

Edwards and Master entered their old one-room office from where they launched the landmark, 'It affects us' movement.

'You still visit this office, Siddharth,' smiled Edwards looking around and reminiscing some cherished memories.

'Very rarely, Edwards. It is still, however, my branch office for Master's Consultancy,' smiled Master.

'There's some magic in this place, Siddharth. I can't express it in words. All I can say is, it somehow opens up your mind and makes you see things a lot clearer,' he said.

'How time flies,' romanticised Master. 'Seems yesterday, when we were sitting on the same study table, same couch and were coining the words "It affects us", he said.

'Yes it has been quite a journey for you from "It affects us" to Goa 2.0,' stated Edwards with a slight hunch, as he helped himself with some tea.

Taking a sip of his black coffee, Master asked, '"It affects us" to "Goa 2.0", doesn't seem right to you or what.'

'It's not about being right, Master. It's about a degree of connect between the two. I don't see that. Stand-alone if you talk, Goa 2.0 is an eye-ball grabbing slogan, no doubt,' said Edwards.

'That perhaps is the social activist in you speaking,' brushed aside Master as he continued. 'Just for the record Edwards, yes Goa 2.0 talks about economic reforms and infrastructure upgradation, etc. but never have I compromised on the inclusiveness of it. Our plans, our initiatives will reach everyone including the least denominator of the society.'

'That's not the point, Siddharth. Look Siddharth, I'm out there in the thick of action in Goa and trust me when I say, Goa doesn't need any overhauling vision or revamping of epic proportions,' said Edwards, trying hard to explain.

'Three years back when you told everyone—It affects us, everyone said—Oh yes, it affects us. You nailed it then,' he said

'Today when you tell me, it's time for Goa 2.0, I say—Ah, may be. And then minutes later, I realize—Hey maybe not, I don't really need all this pompous and extravagant revamping, so to say,' articulated Edwards.

'Then what really does Goa need today?' asked Master.

'They need governance, Master. They need a few stitches here, a few stitches there, some plug-ins, some dial-ups, all in all some good old streamlining and fine-tuning.'

The words struck an instant bell with Master who for

the remaining part of the coffee, sounded very despondent. However, he remained all ears to Edwards till the bottom of his cup.

Master thought long and hard on his drive to Menezes' office who had called for an urgent briefing. As Master got down from the car and made his way in, he was mobbed by the local paparazzi. Pushing, nudging and literally throwing their mikes at Master, they were looking for a fresh set of bytes.

'Master, how's your campaign going?' asked one of them.

'It's going great,' answered Siddharth.

'Jack is going all out, do we expect that from you?' Master laughed it out and said, 'He's an old friend. But seems to me, he's in a bit of an identity crisis.'

'Sir, but you can't deny that he will give you some serious competition,' posed another journalist.

Master, cool as a cucumber said, 'I actually can deny it because quite frankly, Jack is no competition. And I'm not in any way trying to downsize him. It's just that I trust the acumen of the electorate in Goa. They'll not settle down for someone who is yet to settle down in his own life.'

And for the first time, Master actually got a bit harsh on Jack. Maybe Edwards' words were playing on his mind or maybe the competition was just beginning to heat up. Anyway, completing this tete-a-tete with the journalist, he entered the office for the meeting called up by Menezes in the early hours of the morning. As Master entered, he saw Vincent sitting in one corner having a smoke and a panic-struck Menezes walking up and down in the office.

'Master, this is not working. You see the way Jack is making inroads, is kind of alarming. He's on radio, on TV, in clubs and everywhere. Yes I know, our strategy has been to maintain your enigma and not to overexpose but then I guess it needs to change,' he said.

Master tried to calm him and said, 'Look Menezes, I understand what Jack is doing here and frankly, I knew this would happen but the worst thing we can do here is play the game by his rules. Believe me, that's what he wants. Let him do that, as far as we are concerned, let's put our heads together to make this Sunday rally a blockbuster.'

'But, Master, Jack is like 24x7 out there in the centre, meeting people, listening to them, talking to them. I mean, I'm bothered about that, to be honest,' Menezes voiced his concern.

Master heard him carefully and said, 'Menezes, there's nothing we can do about that. You see we can't win this election by wooing and charming people. That is Jack's arena and nobody can touch him there. The only way we can win is by convincing people that yours' truly isn't even in competition with Jack. The people have to be convinced that Jack is not even in his league. And for this, it's important we don't overdo, but whatever little we do is exceptional and on top of that is the Sunday event I'm talking about.'

With seven days to go, Goa was all braced up for two giant rallies scheduled side by side. There were repeated attempts by both parties to negotiate different slots but none of them budged.

Jack's judicious usage of every prior professional connect of his had become an absolute game changer. Meanwhile, in some key pockets like City Centre and Calangute, it was all Master. The labour class swore by him and the upper class intellectuals weren't even ears to someone else's name besides him.

Press releases, media statements were all flying across to and fro like arrows in some old mythology war scene, as it all came down to Sunday.

The Goa Democratic Front's office was bustling with energy. There was a consistent to and fro communication between the City Centre and the party office. Inside the meeting room, everybody looked pumped up and prepared for their last hurrah before the polls.

'What's the status like at the City Centre?' asked Vincent to a couple of party executives as he barged out to the lobby for a quick check-up with the planning team.

Menezes too was continuously over the phone giving last minute instructions. He was heard telling the ground staff to distribute the Goa 2.0 skull caps and merchandise. Meanwhile, Sakshi too walked in, all ready and set to accompany Master. As Menezes hung up the phone and Vincent came back in, Master spoke out with a pause, 'Vincent…Menezes…I won't be talking about Goa 2.0 today.'

A bit surprised Menezes said, 'But that's pretty much our plan, Siddharth. You coined it.'

'Yes, and today I only say that it's not a good idea,' declared Master after carefully thinking it over.

Vincent sharply reacted, 'What are you talking, Siddharth. Goa 2.0 is trending all over the place from the internet to the merchandise at City Centre. It won you the debate against Jack and suddenly you want to toss it out.'

'Whatever, I'm not convinced about it anymore and I'm not speaking about it today,' said Master refusing to budge.

Vincent and Menezes looked in despair and disgust as suddenly this last minute disagreement put the room in a slightly panic mode. Sakshi tried to understand Master's thought behind this and politely asked, 'Siddharth, Goa 2.0 has been your vision, your idea all through. Are you sure you don't want to talk about it?'

Siddharth didn't bat an eyelid and said, 'Look, I'm man enough to moot my own idea and today as I stand, I'm absolutely sure that I don't want to talk about Goa 2.0.'

Vincent and Master were livid and before they could say anything, Rishi entered in and told them it was time to leave. They didn't argue any further and brushing aside the disagreement, they had one final huddle.

'It has been an honour working with you all,' said Menezes.

'Honour is mine, Menezes. I would've never given this a shot, had it not been for you. The respect you people have given me, the trust you've had in me…can't ask for anything more,' said an overwhelmed Siddharth.

'Don't get all emotional, we have a lot to do. Come Thursday and our actual work begins,' said an optimist Vincent as they all made their way out and headed straight to the City Centre.

Meanwhile, the District Centre was also getting ready for Jack and company.

Jack's promotional blitzkrieg, courtesy his media connects had fuelled the already roof-high anticipation. Jack gathered around with his teammates at Joseph's place which was their working office and said, 'Guys, you think I can get the job done?'

'Yes,' came the unanimous reply.

'Let's just hope that's the answer I hear from the people tonight,' said Jack as he also left for the venue that had seen different avatars of his over the years.

As Master arrived at the City Centre, he saw something that rendered him speechless. The Centre was jam-packed to the rafters. It was a display of love and respect people had for Master.

Vincent, Sakshi and Menezes were seated on the makeshift stage as Master walked across to the podium.

The 'Master' chants didn't stop. They got louder with every passing second. So much so that for a good ten minutes, all Master could do was smile and wave-out to them.

It brought back memories of the yesteryears' 'It affects us'. Only this time the passion was replaced by sheer reverence for one individual and that individual today, wasn't a revolutionary economist but an icon who people swore by. It was epic. Master finally did speak out.

'I'm overwhelmed by your affection,' he laughed out to applause.

'15th July, three years back, I told you all or rather you told me three words that changed it forever—It affects us,' pronounced Master in unison with the gathering's voice.

'We've come a long way. As I stand here, before you today, I see a gathering which has given me absolutely everything in life. Support, at a time when I could've very easily wilted and stayed down forever. Love, at a time when death threats, lathi charges and prison terms could've broken me from inside.'

The applause of the people echoed across after every line from Master.

'Assurance, at a time when I myself didn't know for sure whether I'll be able to walk the path we had chosen or not.' Taking a breather and mellowing down, he continued, 'The fact is you people have given me so much that I don't have the courage to ask for more. All I can tell you today, is that come Thursday, if you were to elect me as your MP, I promise I'll give it my 1,000 per cent.' A huge uproar greeted Master's assurance.

'As a little boy, who grew up in the by-lanes of Panjim,

never had I thought, I'd come this far,' he said with a smile and a sense of pride.

'I wasn't born in a very affluent family and neither did I have any Godfather holding my hand, but I just kept walking,' he said.

'I was told by a school teacher that I make little sense when it comes to reasoning and logic but I just kept walking,' reiterated Master building a soaring momentum.

'I became an economist, wanted to start my own consultancy. Nobody, no corporate, no business house gave me a chance, but I just kept walking,' romanticized Master as the people echoed together the common creed, 'I just kept walking.'

'I told the system that it affects us. They said—Not so much, but I...just kept walking,' he said with a greater conviction every time.

He paused for a while and then in a whispering tone, he said, 'I then told the people that I want to be your Member of Parliament. And...you...told me...we're with you but hey, there's also a guy named Jack who's quite good,' laughed off Master with a degree of sarcasm. He then paused for a second, looked around for a while and then with whispering humbleness said, 'Come Thursday, you people will take an important decision. Rather, we'll all take an important decision.'

'Thank you and God bless you all,' cried out Master to one last round of applause as Vincent, Sakshi, Menezes and all others joined him for the final bow.

If overwhelming was the word to describe Master's rally then nailed it would be the one to describe Jack's show.

This banjara had managed to woo a record attendance at the District Centre. The huge open air hall today was witness to his first real show of strength against Master. No one could've ever thought that someone could achieve such numbers against Master in his own yard.

The rally did kick-start with the expected callout, 'Ladies and gentlemen, boys and girls, children of all ages, this is Goa's own Jack saying hello to each one of you.' Once through with the greeting, Jack didn't waste a second in coming to the point.

'A lot of people don't think that I deserve to be in the same league as Master,' said Jack with a rare kind of seriousness. 'Jack's just a wanderer, they say and he shouldn't perhaps even be competing with Master.' Pausing for a second, he continued, 'The fact is, ladies and gentlemen, they are absolutely spot on.' The gathering was abuzz with surprise at Jack's bizarreness.

'The fact is, I don't hold a candle in front of Master and I can't even dream of competing with him. But who I can dream of competing with and defeating fair and square is Siddharth,' declared Jack to a thunderous applause from the crowd.

'So this Thursday is it going to be Siddharth or is it going to be Master, who would I be pitted against? Ironically though, he claims that I have an identity crisis.'

With these words, Jack took the mike in his hand and came out in front leaving the podium.

'The fact is, this Thursday, I'm not stepping up against Master. No! I can't. He's too damn good an economist, a revolutionary and even a dozen Jacks put together can't touch him.'

Getting more serious, Jack continued, 'My opponent this Thursday is a guy who stays in Mumbai, has his heart and soul in economics and his consultancy...but, what he's eyeing is Goa. Now that's pretty unlike Master!'

'That guy's a genius when it comes to policies and numbers,

pretty much a master, but when it comes to the ground reality of what people need, want or require, he quite frankly doesn't know a jack about it,' claimed Jack. 'This Thursday, it's going be Jack versus Siddharth. It's going to be, "I'll stay here and get the job done" versus "I'll keep a check from Mumbai via satellite",' thumped Jack with authority, as he fired one salvo after another.

'It's up to you guys to decide who you want as your Member of Parliament. A guy who might not be that flowery, that scholarly but knows your problem and will get to the root of it or the guy who is an intellectual dynamite but you can't count on to be there,' reasoned Jack.

A brief silence followed by a round of applause spoke volumes about how the audience that day was absorbing every word Jack said.

'This Thursday means everything to me. My entire life's been a build-up to this. Each and every single step of my life, each and every thing I ever did leads to this Thursday. I know, I've done things in the past and left them after a point but God is the witness and Goa is the testimony that I've always risen up and come even closer to you,' stressed Jack with an exuberance laced with raw emotion seeping through every pore of his body. Each and every person in the crowd at that moment could feel the beat of his heart and written across every beat was 'I'll get the job done'.

'Phew…,' breathed out Jack. 'Can't wait for Thursday, guys,' he signed off with his characteristic smile and resigned his fate in the hands of the people.

Without any glitz or glamour that day Jack indeed put up a show like only he could.

Samantha was struggling to hold back her tears. Over the

years, she was always skeptical and proud of Jack at the same time. Well, today she got rid of the former and all she had was pride for her husband.

.15.

This Is It!

The dust finally settled at both the District Centre and the City Centre. Jack and company were literally drained and exhausted after their marathon effort. Master and his camp also took some time off to unwind. The speculative market was in overdrive mode. As the day approached its end, numbers started pouring in.

Vincent and Menezes were both at Master's place when Master confirmed them the numbers forwarded by his office. A whooping 1,386 people had attended Master's rally only to be bettered by a record 1,401 who had gathered for Jack's final hurrah.

'Fourteen hundred and one…can't believe it,' said Menezes sitting in Master's dining room.

Master smiled and said, 'I was watching some excerpts. He really had the ball rolling.'

'That whole Siddharth and Master analogy was pretty original, I must say,' said Master rather sportingly.

'What does your recursive model say, Vincent?' asked Menezes.

'It's going to be real close, Menezes. From what I gather every single vote is going to count, but I'll still give the edge to Master,' he said.

'1,401 to 1,386 doesn't suggest that, does it?' enquired Menezes.

'You see Menezes, this model takes a lot of things into account and the one thing your naked eye's missing is that Master's support base is loyal to death. Jack doesn't enjoy that luxury, quite frankly. People who swear by Master won't even have a second thought in their mind when they're punching the EVM,' reasoned Vincent.

'Vincent...after the last few days and especially today, a lot of people are going to have second thoughts,' said Master.

'That only time will tell, Siddharth. But as far as our model's concerned, you win the Thursday election by a whisker,' said Vincent.

'Whis-ker or whiskey, what's on your mind, Vincent?' laughed out Master making light of the situation.

'Oh sure, we'll open the bottle, this Thursday,' said Menezes.

'Cheers to the thought, though I'm a teetotaler,' smiled Master.

'Should've used that as a selling point in our campaign. Teetotaler Master or tanker Jack?' laughed out Vincent as they all had a nice laugh and a stress-busting evening.

Time, however kept ticking and marching towards the D-day. For one guy, however, it was moving at a snail's pace. Jack was roaming around his household like a zombie. The guy couldn't wait for the big Thursday. Sam walked in and sat next to him outside their sea-facing apartment.

'Fourteen hundred, Jack...can't ask for more, can you?' said Sam.

'I can't Sam, I just can't. To be honest, all I want to do now is just know the result,' he said.

Sam smiled and resting her head on his shoulder said, 'I sometimes miss the Jack who'd just throw caution to the wind and not worry about results or anything.'

Jack sarcastically cleared his cough and said, 'Excuse me, is this Samantha I-dumped-my-wanderer-husband talking?'

'No, this is Samantha I-fell-in-love-with-a-wanderer-and-got-married talking,' she winked mischievously.

'Oh…I get it, so sometimes you need a reckless exploring banjara and then, there are times when you need a seasoned, mature responsible man,' asked Jack in his tongue-in-cheek manner.

Sam got her head up from his shoulder, thought for a second, 'Hmmm' and then said, 'Oh absolutely and do you have a problem?' she asserted fiercely and yet so affectionately.

Jack said, 'Not at all sweetie, post Thursday, I'll work like a responsible individual all day and in the night, we'll hop around and run crazy races,' he laughed.

Sam too gently smiled and the two passionately shared a moment of love and togetherness. After a few minutes Sam sitting hand in hand with Jack, said to him, 'Honey, this Thursday, I want you to be prepared for anything, you understand me?'

'Oh…Sam, I've never been more prepared for anything in my life. As long as you're there with me, nothing is going to bother me,' as the two affectionately kissed.

'Unless, tomorrow I get an offer to become a bungee jumping instructor in Hawaii…,' he said pulling her leg.

She affectionately elbowed him in the stomach and appeared pissed as Jack, very lovingly began cajoling her. The sea in front looked quite calm and was in sharp contrast to the underlying tension which was building up with every passing minute.

Minutes did however pass and so did the hours and so did the couple of days. It all, however stopped on that Thursday which was going to decide their fate

The media frenzy that day was madness to say the least. Away from their glare and away from any sort of vile speculation, Master had early morning left for his old study office at Pedal Street.

There were over ten voting centres established in the constituency itself. The press, the party representatives and even the common man of Goa, were all set for what was believed to be one of the most closely contested polls ever. The poll turnout in that constituency was a record.

The Election Commission Office was in complete overdrive mode. Different party representatives had been dropping in to check up the proceedings for the polls. Vincent and Menezes paid a visit early morning and cast their votes as soon as the booth opened after the clock ticked 8 a.m. Sakshi and Master's parents too followed up in sometime.

Every Goan who entered the booth that day had numerous voices speaking out loud in their mind. From the stirring and compelling "It affects us" to the definitive and resolute "I'll get the job done". From the ever so enticingly dreamy Goa 2.0 to the assuredly pragmatic Goa Fine-tuned".

For the people it was down to which sound was louder, which visual elicited more emotion and most importantly who did they see or who did they hear as their Member of Parliament, as the raised finger committed its seemingly few inches long journey to punch the EVM.

As the day progressed, Goa saw everyone important to the two, turn up one by one. Francis Edwards, the social activist, Joseph from Grinnel's, A.N. Mistry, the man who conceived the whole Jack and politics marriage, Samantha and not to mention Jack himself turned up and as the evening set in, the shutterbugs finally also got to see Master, who till now was strangely conspicuous by his absence.

His car stopped right outside the voting centre and out he came all alone and all by himself. He didn't oblige the shutterbugs much nor did he give any requested bytes. His characteristic swagger was there but a bit restrained, a bit withdrawn as Master step by step inched towards the polling booth.

'So who won, who made it to the finish line?' Master asked the gathering at India Gate which was on tenterhooks for this one. Master looked around at the people and smiled and then for a second, what flashed right across his mind was a visual he would never forget. Master didn't talk about that visual to the crowd in front, however the flashes in his mind continued beneath the silence. The flashing visual started from the time Master parked his car that day, right outside the polling booth. The blurred flashes continued as Master remembered how he got down from the car and looked around at the journalists standing there pressing for some bytes. Master distinctly remembered how at that moment he was pretty much in his own orbit, in his own world He then reached the polling booth and stared long and hard at the EVM machine. And then Master's finger did hit the button, the button representing his rival Jack. Oh yes Master voted for Jack. This reality remained buried in Master's heart. It was something neither the Hall of Fame audience nor anyone else would ever know. Meanwhile the crowd at India Gate was getting restless with anticipation as Master's silence continued killing them.

'It was Jack,' shouted out Master and after a euphoria from

certain sections, he quietly said, 'by one vote...phew.'

Jack won by one singular solitary vote. The thought had so many layers to it. Everybody knew it'd be close, but this close was something that made them smile, made them crazy and quite frankly thrilled them to the point of an adrenaline knock-out.

Narrating this had been an emotionally draining experience for Master as well and it wasn't long before the smile on his face was adorned by a few tears of joy in his eyes and soon everybody stood up on their feet and gave it all they had for the man. For those three hours, each and every one of them had lived, breathed, sensed and smelt every drop of blood, sweat and tears of Jack and Master.

'One vote...one freaking vote,' the mention kept popping up amongst the people, as they seemed to sink in the sheer emotion this fact carried. Little did they know that all they knew was perhaps just the tip of an iceberg of emotions this fact entailed.

.16.

Master's Inner Thoughts

Prof Bhaskar's lecture, question no. 3, my first research paper.

Seems yesterday, though actually it happened some twenty years ago. That day, my paper laid to rest many doubts, many theories and many questions, except for one. Ironically, though that one question was raised by none other than Jack himself. Little did we know about the symbolic relevance that question would have in our lives.

'Do economists make for good politicians?' was that question and to this day, I don't have a definitive answer and neither do I think Jack has. What I do, however, have today is perhaps a fair idea of who makes for a better politician—a 'Jack' or a 'Master'?

I know today for sure that only and only a 'Master' can build a masterpiece, but the society needs a 'Jack' to ensure the right place of that masterpiece in the larger scheme of things.

I also know today that a 'Master' toils his butt off and dives into the depths of his craft to come out with jewels of rare quality, like only he can. However, at times it takes the gifted quality of a 'Jack', to choose that one jewel which shall be the shining glory of a crown.

Back then, I did dive into the depths of my passion and came out with the vision Goa 2.0. However, as time passed and the cloud of passion cleared away, I realized that Jack's 'Goa

Fine-tuned was indeed the relevant jewel, for the crowning glory of Goa. I realized that Goa politics at that point didn't need a 'Master', what they needed was a people's representative, what they needed was a 'Jack'.

Siddharth or Master? I don't know what they make of me. It were the people or to be specific it was Jack, who gave me the title 'Master'. I never really thought of myself as one but from where I see it, that day on the 21st of November the man who punched the button on the EVM was not Siddharth but Master.

.17.

It Really Was a Tiger!

'*Phew...*,' *breathed out Master and then reiterated the creed that perhaps summed up his life,* '*And...I just kept walking...*'

'*Three years later, Master's Consultancy Pvt. Ltd was listed on the Bombay stock exchange and it won the Golden Biz Honour Award for excellence. Six years later, I became one of the advisory members of the Planning Commission, Mumbai and ten years later, I sit before you today as the Financial Advisor to the Prime Minister.*'

The claps, the chants and the unabashed reverence kept coming in as Master with a complacent smile said, '*That's it guys. Thank you so much and on a lighter note God bless the guy who's been this late and allowed us this much time.*'

With these words, Master for the one final time waved out to the gathering at India Gate, as the announcer for the evening came back on stage and gave him a warm hug.

Just as Master was getting up from the couch, the announcer called out loud, 'Master...Master.' Master looked around and wondered. The announcer smiled and said, 'Sir, you don't need to go absolutely anywhere.' The smile, by now had reached the man's ears as he looked towards the crowd and said, 'Ladies and gentlemen, our second inductee in the Hall of Fame...'

The announcer paused for a while and then in a resounding

euphoria called out loud, 'Can you believe it, is none other than Goa's own Jack.'

It blew the roof off at India Gate. An absolute mayhem of a celebration and excitement had gripped the place. Master couldn't stop smiling and neither could the hundred plus who just had an out of body experience.

And then, out came the quintessential charmer, the banjara, Goa's own and most recently Governor Jack. Oh yes, in a casual white shirt and blue denims, Governor Jack was in the house and the first person he met was Master.

'This is truly their Everest,' shouted out the announcer amidst thunderous applause and claps galore.

Catching his breath back, the announcer in a lighter vein said, 'As happy we are to see you here, Jack that doesn't stop us from complaining about the three hours, you kept us waiting.' Jack then walked towards the centre stage, grabbed the microphone and said, 'Guys, you know what there's a reason why I'm late.'

The gathering laughed out loud and they bloody well knew what was coming up next.

'Guys, on my way here, I was actually chased.'

'By a tiger,' completed the gathering as they laughed out loud.

Jack couldn't believe, they knew it and with a smile, he carried on, 'I would've killed him but then my eyes fell on the sponsor hoarding—Save the tiger, only 1,411 are left.'

The crowd laughed out loud as Jack winked towards them. He then turned around towards Master and said, 'Can't believe you told them this...'

The two had a nice laugh and so did the gathering. However once the laughter settled and sanity returned, Jack held the microphone and said, 'Fact is ladies and gentlemen, I'm glad, I reached here (pointing to the Hall of Fame couch) only after Master, because frankly that's how it should be. Truth is that a Jack perhaps can pull off any string in the world, but it takes a Master to touch the chord of greatness.'

Acknowledgements

So here we go, this finally is happening. What you're holding in your hand would've remained a figment of my imagination had it not been for some amazingly selfless people in my life:

I begin by thanking my Mom. Every word, every comma, every full stop in this book is an ode to her effort in bringing me up. *Jack & Master* above everything else is my little way of saying a big thank you to my mother. Thank you, Mom for teaching me every essay, every poem and every lesson while I was growing up.

Next up is my Dad. I'm blessed to have such an encouraging and chilled out father. I must've been eight years old, when he once told me, 'Karan, you can do anything in this world if you set your heart and mind on it'. Those words have and will always stay with me.

My sister, Divya is and will always be the superstar of our family. She is one person I never mind getting my butt kicked by. Her affection, her goodness and her inner strength puts perennial cribbers and spoilt jacks like me to shame.

My maternal uncle, Viki Mama is someone with whom I've played everything from wrestling to pakda-pakdi to golf and what not.

I also thank my Nana and Nani. I am blessed to have them in my life.

Jasmeet Singh, the man who personifies the adage 'Friend in need is a friend in deed'. Thanks a ton!

Feroz, the first person who told me that *Jack & Master* will go very far.

Alok Mishra, a friend who I know will always give me the most sincere advice in life!

Ali Abbas, the player 2 of every single Nintendo, PS2, XBOX game I've played.

Nitin and Mohit, two amazing people I met a little late in life but thank God we met.

A shout-out to my gang at college—Shobhit, Bhalla, Ankit, Nalin, Varun and Brijendra. Thanks for the support!

Mr Pradeep Chhabra for his encouragement at a time most needed.

The team at Rupa Publications for bringing this together.

Jack & Master is a gift to me from the Almighty. So I thank you God and I promise you I'll do whatever justice I can with the craft you've given me.